Annabelle moved to brush by him, but he caught her arm, stopping her, forcing her to look at him.

She felt the heat of his fingers to the very center of her being. "Take your hand off me!"

Rush tightened his grip. "Why? Because I'm the hired help?"

Anna cocked up her chin. Furious. With him. With herself, for allowing him to get to her, for almost kissing him before. For wishing he'd kiss her now. "Yes," she lied. "Because you're the hired help."

"You are one cold princess."

"And I could fire you."

"You could." He smiled, the curving of his lips slow and confident. "But you won't."

"Are you so sure?"

His gaze lowered to her mouth for one dizzying moment, and then he lifted it back to her eyes. "Yes. You need me, Anna. You hate it, but it's true...."

Dear Reader,

Welcome to Silhouette *Special Edition* . . . welcome to romance.

Last year I requested your opinions on the books that we publish. Thank you for the many thoughtful comments. Throughout the past months I've been sharing quotes from these letters with you. This seems very appropriate while we are in the midst of our THAT SPECIAL WOMAN! promotion, as each of our readers is a very special woman.

This month, our THAT SPECIAL WOMAN! is Lt. Callie Donovan, a woman whose military career is on the line. Lindsay McKenna brings you this story of determination and love in *Point of Departure*.

Also this month is *Forever* by Ginna Gray, another book in the BLAINES AND THE McCALLS OF CROCKETT, TEXAS series. Erica Spindler brings you *Magnolia Dawn,* the second book in her BLOSSOMS OF THE SOUTH series. And don't miss Sherryl Woods's *A Daring Vow*— a tie-in to her VOWS series—as well as stories from Andrea Edwards and Jean Ann Donathan.

I hope you enjoy this book, and all of the stories to come!

Sincerely,

Tara Gavin
Senior Editor

QUOTE OF THE MONTH:

"I have an MA in Humanities. I like to read funny and spirited stories. I really enjoy novels set in distinctive parts of the country with strong women and equally strong men. . . . Please continue to publish books that are delightful to read. Nothing is as much fun as finding a great story. I will continue to buy books that entertain and make me smile."

—T. Kanowith, Maryland

ERICA
SPINDLER

MAGNOLIA DAWN

Silhouette®

SPECIAL EDITION®

Published by Silhouette Books

America's Publisher of Contemporary Romance

For Jan (Celeste Hamilton) Powell who gave me the phrase,
"He sets my panties on fire."
Who but a true blossom of the South
could have come up with this?

Thanks for sharing your Southern experiences with me. But more,
thanks for being such a good friend.

And for the women of Delta State University (especially Maryanne
Ross, Terry Simmons, Lilah Perry and Maxine Meriweather)
who gave me my first taste of what being a
Southern woman is all about.

SILHOUETTE BOOKS

RECYCLED PAPER

ISBN 0-373-09857-X

MAGNOLIA DAWN

Copyright © 1993 by Erica Spindler

Books by Erica Spindler

Silhouette Special Edition

Longer Than... #696
Baby Mine #728
*A Winter's Rose #817
*Night Jasmine #838
*Magnolia Dawn #857

Silhouette Desire

Heaven Sent #442
Chances Are #482
Read Between the Lines #538

*Blossoms of the South

ERICA SPINDLER

believes in love at first date. Because that's all the time it took for her and her husband, Nathan, to fall in love. "We were too young. We both had to finish college. Our parents thought we should see other people, but we knew we were meant for each other," Erica says. Thirteen years later, they still know it.

Erica chose her home—Louisiana—the same way. She went "way down yonder" for a visit, fell in love with the state and decided to stay. "I may have been born in the Midwest," she says, "but I'm a true Southerner at heart." It is that continuing love affair with the people and customs of the South that inspired Erica to write her Blossoms of the South trilogy.

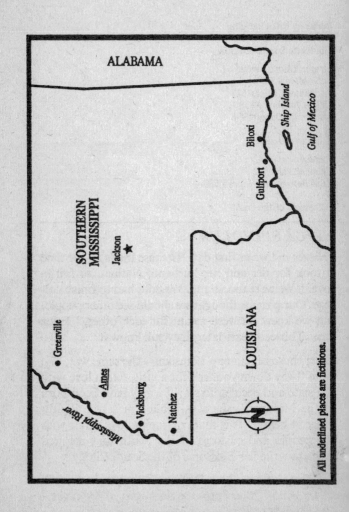

ALABAMA

Ship Island

Gulf of Mexico

Biloxi

Gulfport

SOUTHERN
MISSISSIPPI

Jackson

Greenville

Ames

Vicksburg

Natchez

Mississippi River

LOUISIANA

All underlined places are fictitious.

Prologue

Small Miracles occupied the first floor of a pristine brownstone on Boston's trendy Boylston Street. Rush Cousins gazed at the building, then checked the address again. The proprietor of Small Miracles had called on his firm to quote a renovation to the brownstone, but from where he stood, the building didn't even need to be cleaned. He shook his head. Maybe the inside told a different story. Rush crossed the street, smiling at a woman in a miniskirt as she gave him an appreciative once-over. After a last glance, he climbed the steps to the shop's door. Before he'd even finished ringing the buzzer, a woman who reminded him of a cross between a good fairy and a leprechaun opened the door.

"You must be Rush," she said, smiling brilliantly. "I'm Marla." She threw the door wide. "Welcome to Small Miracles."

Rush returned Marla's smile, instantly liking the little woman. She radiated enthusiasm and zest for life. "It's good to meet you, Marla."

"You, too." She rubbed her hands together. "I've been anxious for you to get here so we could get started. This is terribly exciting. Don't you think?"

Rush laughed. "I do like my work, Marla. Especially renovations." He stepped across the threshold and into the antique shop, looking over the interior as he did. "Although I have to say, this place is in great shape. I don't know what you have in mind, but—"

She stopped him with a fluttery motion of her right hand. "Fiddle-dee-dee. Don't give *that* a second thought."

Rush lifted his eyebrows in amusement. Obviously money wasn't an issue here. Neither was logic. "How did you hear about Cousins's Building and Restorations?"

Marla met his eyes. Hers were the clearest blue he'd ever seen. Looking into them was like gazing up at the cloudless heavens. Her lips curved as with a private joke. "Your name popped up, Mr. Cousins. And I took it." As he opened his mouth to ask where it had 'popped up,' she added, "Do you know much about antiques?"

"No." He swept his gaze over the room. "But I do admire their craftsmanship. Most people are more concerned with quantity than quality. That's too bad, I think." He slipped his hands into the front pockets of his blue jeans and tipped his head toward the ceiling, admiring the ornate ceiling medallion above him. "That's why I love these old places. They fascinate me, really."

Marla beamed at him. "A perfectly wonderful answer."

Rush laughed again. "Was I taking a test?"

Marla laughed, too, then clucked her tongue. "All we do today is hurry. What's the sense of it? For myself, I believe the really good things in life take time. Have a look around, Mr. Cousins. I'll get us coffee."

She started for the back of the store, then paused and looked over her shoulder at him. Her blue eyes twinkled with amusement. "Pay special attention to the items on the Chippendale side table behind you. They're very special."

"Thanks. I'll do that." Smiling again, Rush swung around, his thoughts moving to the day ahead. After this appointment, he was meeting the contractor in charge of the Fairfield job. Before he did, he needed to call Joe about the invoices in ques—

Rush's thoughts stopped short. On the table Marla had mentioned sat one item only, a domed music box. Its workmanship and materials were top-notch—lavish, even. A glass dome rested on a luminous wood base decorated with gold filigree. Inside the dome, a porcelain replica of a Southern belle in a billowing hoop skirt and picture hat held a bunch of flowers.

Rush sucked in a sharp breath, a sense of recognition balling in his chest, fighting his heart and lungs for space.

He'd seen this music box before.

Drawing his eyebrows together, he racked his brain for the time, the place, he recognized this object from. But even as he did, Rush acknowledged his effort as wasted. His memory of this thing came from his shadows, from the time before St. Catherine's Orphanage and the Sisters who had taken him in, a time before the string of foster homes or his days of living on the street. This memory came from a place and time he knew but couldn't quite touch.

Rush reached for the box and closed his hands carefully around it. The feel of it was like a shock to his system. His head filled with sensory memories—of heat and moisture and of a slow, even languorous pace. And with the smell of flowers, rich and ripe and sweet.

His hands began to shake. Oh, yes, he had seen this box before. He had held it, just like this, sometime, somewhere in his past.

Even as he told himself his thoughts were ludicrous, Rush turned the small gold key at the box's back. A moment before the tune began to play, its lilting notes filled his head.

"Son of a bitch," he whispered, his hands shaking in earnest now, his heart thundering against the wall of his chest. It couldn't be. But it was.

In his hands he held a clue to his past.

His past, Rush thought again, stunned. That cavernous space whose faceless shadows and intangible sensations had been a part of him for as long as he could clearly remember.

He drew in a sharp breath. Why now? he wondered, watching the tiny belle as she circled the base. He'd grown accustomed to being a man whose past didn't exist before age five. He no longer cared why he'd been abandoned or by whom. He had been; those were the facts of his life. Knowing his past wouldn't change them. It wouldn't change the man he'd become.

"Here we are," Marla called brightly. She set a tray laden with a silver coffee service down on a table in front of a dainty-looking settee. "Oh, good. I see you've found the box."

Rush frowned. "Where did you get this?"

"Excuse me?"

"The box," he said, trying to harness his impatience. "Do you know where it's from?"

"Of course," she answered mildly, as if not at all surprised by his interest—or sudden surliness. She sank onto the settee. "Don't worry, Mr. Cousins. I will tell you everything you need to know. But first..." she patted the space next to her "...sit and have a cup of coffee."

Although every fiber of his being urged action, Rush did as she asked. Marla filled a translucent china cup with coffee, then handed it to him. The tiny cup felt awkward in his big hand, and he set it down. "The music box," he prompted, the impatience pushing at him, refusing to be quieted.

"Ah, yes. It's lovely, isn't it?" Marla took a sip of her coffee, then patted her mouth with a napkin. "The box is from a Mississippi plantation named Ashland. Have you heard of it?" When he shook his head in the negative, she continued. "Ashland was one of the great Mississippi plantations. And also one of the few plantation homes to remain in the hands of its original family."

She lifted her shoulders. "Although there are now only two descendants left, a brother and a sister. They're having a difficult time keeping the house up and have been forced to sell off the plantation's furnishings and other family heirlooms. Like the music box. Sad," she finished, taking another sip of her coffee. "Tragic, really."

Ashland, Rush thought, testing the sound of it in his head. He expected some sort of bell of recognition to ring, some shock similar to the one he'd experienced

when he'd seen the music box. Instead, he drew a
blank.

He made a sound of frustration. "Where in Mississippi is ... Ashland?"

"Ames. Between Vicksburg and Greenville, in the
Delta. The town was named after the plantation family. That's the way it was often done in those days."

It sounded so familiar, Rush thought. And so foreign. Did he recognize these names, this story? Or did
he merely want to? He shifted his gaze, looking once
again at the music box. His recognition of the box
wasn't a fabrication of his imagination. He'd known its
tune before it had played. He *had* held that box in his
hands sometime in his past. Unless ...

Rush looked at Marla. "Is it possible that there's
another music box exactly like this one? Or at least one
that's similar but plays the same tune? Could there—"

"Oh, dear, no." Marla shook her head and her ri-
otous red curls bounced against her cheeks. "This
music box was commissioned for the third mistress of
Ashland. It's a one-of-a-kind."

Rush sat back. What would he find if he went there,
to Ames, Mississippi, and Ashland Plantation? Would
he once and for all learn the truth about those lost five
years of his life? Or would he find ... nothing? More
shadows?

Memories of his childhood—these crystal-clear and
razor-sharp—filled his head. Memories of the times
before he'd understood the rules; times when he'd
barreled in, his heart and hope on the line, and had
been coldly turned away. He'd promised himself he
would never be that kind of fool again.

What he was considering was ridiculous. After all,
what would he say to the brother and sister of Ash-

land? Hi, I think I may belong here. By any chance are you missing a family member? And how would these owners of Ashland respond? Sure, come on in. Help yourself to the family silver.

Right. Rush curled his hands into fists. He didn't need to know his past. It didn't matter. He'd long ago let go of the yearning to know who he was and where he'd come from.

"Fascinating, isn't it?" Marla murmured, interrupting his thoughts. "How sometimes in finding the past we learn our future."

Rush looked at the woman, his pulse beating slowly and heavily in his head. "What did you say?"

She smiled, and again he was caught by the cloudless yet mesmerizing blue of her eyes. "That you seem a man whose instincts are good, Rush Cousins. I think you should follow them."

Chapter One

A week later Rush stood at the entrance to Ashland, the unrelenting June sun beating down on the road beneath his feet, the heat emanating back up at him in invisible waves. Behind him the Mississippi River flowed peacefully, yet the levee facing it served as a stark reminder of its unpredictable and often-violent moods.

Before him, a grove of magnolias stretched from the road to the house, lining the pathway that led to Ashland Plantation, creating a living canopy of green. The magnificent trees, easily six feet in diameter, were in full bloom, their dark, glossy tops dotted with huge white blossoms. Even from his position beyond the grove, Rush could smell their ripe, sweet scent.

He turned his gaze from the magnolias to the house, visible at the end of the alleyway of trees. The huge Greek Revival structure rose up from the ground to dominate all around it. A living vision of the past, looking at it brought to mind romantic stories of the Old South, of ladies and gentlemen and codes of honor. And it brought to mind other stories—bloody ones imbued with neither romance nor glory.

Rush stared at the house, a dozen different emotions churning inside him. Awe at its magnificence. Admiration for its beauty, for its having endured the ravages of war and weather and social changes that made it both object of beauty and picture of corruption.

But déjà vu? Rush shook his head, frustrated. He couldn't say for sure.

A woman stepped out onto the gallery. From this distance Rush could make out nothing of her except her sex, and that, only because of the light-colored dress she wore and the way the wind caught the fabric and billowed it around her knees.

Annabelle Ames, he thought. Mistress of Ashland. He'd been in Ames nearly a week, posing as a drifter. As is the way in small towns, people had been only too eager to gossip. He'd learned much about Annabelle and Lowell Ames. Many of the things he'd learned had been less than flattering.

They'd called her a spinster. They'd described her as plain and prim as a Sunday morning, but kind and hardworking, as well. She taught first-graders at the local grammar school, and the children loved her; she could be a bit uppity if she didn't get her way, and downright regal if crossed.

And she was obsessed with saving her family home. She'd devoted her life to it, spending every free moment—and every spare cent—on its upkeep. They thought her crazy for her obsession.

Of course her brother Lowell, they'd said, was no good at all.

Looking at Annabelle Ames now, at the picture she made standing alone on the veranda of that glorious house, something stirred inside him. Something bittersweet and dangerously close to emotions he'd felt before. Ones like longing. Like alienation.

Rush frowned and hiked his duffel bag higher on his shoulder, conscious of the music box carefully wrapped and tucked inside. It wouldn't do to forget the lessons of his past. It wouldn't do to allow himself to feel too much. He'd come to Ashland for answers, plain and simple. And if, indeed, there were any here for him, he would find them.

Rush tightened his mouth in determination. Annabelle Ames was looking for a handyman to help her make repairs to Ashland. According to Bubba at the Feed and Seed, she'd had no takers and was getting desperate. The same as every year.

Rush smiled and started for the house. Today was going to be Annabelle Ames's lucky day.

Annabelle drew in a lungful of the morning air, heavy with the pungency of summer. Yesterday at this time she'd been in a classroom, trying to contain a group of six-year-olds who knew the next day would be their first of summer vacation. And doing it while her own thoughts had been just as focused on the summer ahead.

Annabelle smiled, relishing the freedom of her first day, looking forward to spending the days and weeks ahead at Ashland. The people in town, her friends and colleagues, even her own brother, thought her love of

Ashland strange, thought her determination to save it more than a little crazy.

She knew the things they said about her, knew what they called her. She shook her head and moved her gaze over the view before her, taking in the ancient live oaks, draped in Spanish moss, the gardens, wildly overgrown but still thick with azaleas, camellias and gardenias, the classical fountain, its cherubs desperately in need of repair but deliciously whimsical.

Ashland was her home—it had been home to six generations of Ameses. Everything about this place struck a chord of beauty and peace inside her.

But how could she explain that to her critics? How could she verbalize the way Ashland made her feel or how much preserving it meant to her?

She couldn't; she'd tried. Annabelle smiled. Let them think what they would; their opinions meant nothing to her.

Except for Lowell's. Her smile faded and she leaned against one of the massive columns, its plaster cool and damp despite the warmth of the sun. What had she done to make her brother resent her so? How could they have veered so far apart that they couldn't even speak to one another without arguing?

Sadness curled through her. And regret. They were family, all that the other had left. If only they could be close, the way they once had been.

If only she could make him happy.

Anna forcefully turned her thoughts from ones of her brother to ones of Ashland and the job she had to do. She had the summer, only three short months, to undo the damage of nine. A meager one hundred and twenty days to keep destruction from Ashland's front doors. And an even more meager amount of money to do it with.

She had to begin repairs, handyman or not. She drew in a deep breath. Skilled help would make a world of difference in what she could accomplish this summer. With someone who knew what they were doing, she could get two, maybe three times the repairs done that she had last year with the high-school student she'd hired.

But where would she find help like that when she had only minimum wage to offer?

A man appeared from beneath the magnolia canopy, and Anna straightened. He walked toward her, his stride long and brisk. From this distance he looked big and powerfully built. Dressed casually, in worn blue jeans and white T-shirt, he had a duffel bag flung over his shoulder.

Anna sensed his gaze upon her, although he didn't call out or lift his hand in greeting. Her heart began to thrum, her palms to sweat. She knew everyone in Ames; she'd never seen this man before.

Anna took a step back from the gallery railing. The river and hundreds of acres of undeveloped land isolated Ashland Plantation from the rest of the community, and she was absolutely alone here.

Turning, she strode to the door and whistled. A moment later Blue, her black Labrador retriever, shot through the door. He caught the stranger's scent immediately, and growled low in his throat.

"Good boy," Anna whispered, slipping her fingers through his collar to hold him at her side. She crossed to the steps and waited for the stranger.

The man stopped at the bottom of the stairs and tipped his face up to hers. Her first thought was that he reminded her of Blue, big and brawny and deceptively fierce. Her second was that he was handsome, in a brash, outdoorsy way. His sandy hair was thick and almost wavy; his eyes, a rich hazel, were creased at the corners from years of amusement or squinting against the sun. Although a man of her age, there was something boyish in his demeanor, as if he laughed often and enjoyed life fully.

As she silently assessed him, he smiled. The lifting of his lips, slow and somehow cocky, cut a deep dimple in his right cheek. The smile transformed his face from handsome to irresistible. And transformed him from an ordinary man to a charming rogue. A sexy rascal. The kind of man who made her feel awkward and plain.

The kind of man a woman should never trust. Especially a woman like herself.

"Good morning," he said, his dimple deepening. "By any chance are you Annabelle Ames?"

Not only big and handsome, but Yankee, too. She silently swore. "By any chance," she replied haughtily, "can I help you?"

"Maybe." He smiled again. "But maybe it's I who can help you."

She tightened her fingers around Blue's collar, but arched her eyebrows coolly. "Is that so?"

He laughed and climbed the stairs to stop before her. He held out his hand. "Rush Cousins. I've come about the job."

Annabelle gazed at his outstretched hand a moment, then placed hers in his. His fingers closed over hers gently, yet she could feel their strength. His skin was warm against hers, his palm callused. His touch made her feel small and vulnerable. And trapped.

Heart thundering, she slipped her hand from his. He seemed not to notice her discomfort, and crossed to one of the columns, to a place where the plaster had chipped away to reveal the understructure of mud and brick. "Beautiful place," he murmured. "Must be a devil to keep up."

"Or a joy," she countered. "Do you know much about the construction of plantation homes?"

"I've done some reading about them. Recently." He moved his fingers over the column. Although he was big and rough looking, there seemed something gentle, almost tender, about the way he explored the surface of the column.

"Then you'll know that all the bricks were made right here on the plantation."

"From river clay," he finished for her. "The mortar is an incredibly durable combination of moss and mud. As I understand it, except in rare cases, only indigenous materials were used in building plantations. River clay, moss, cypress and oak." He moved his fingers over the surface again, and again she caught herself staring at them. "Fascinating stuff."

She dragged her gaze away. "I don't recognize you, Mr. Cousins. How did you hear about the job?"

He crossed back to her. Taking a folded paper from his T-shirt pocket, he handed it to her. "From this." Anna didn't have to unfold it to know it was one of her Help Wanted signs. She took it anyway.

"I saw it in Bubba's front window," he continued. "I only arrived in Ames a week ago."

"Really? From where?"

"Boston."

As if sensing his master's unease, Blue growled again. Anna put her hand on Blue's head, to reassure the animal, but also to remind the man that she wasn't alone. Rush Cousins didn't seem a bit concerned, even though the dog could rip him to shreds, given the word.

"Bubba said you were anxious to find someone."

Anna frowned, wanting to throttle the loquacious Bubba Percell. "Did he?"

"Called you desperate, actually."

Embarrassed color heated her cheeks. *Desperate.* The images that word brought forth—ones that had nothing to do with finding a handyman—stung. That's how the people of Ames thought of her. And she had no doubt that that was how they'd described her to this stranger.

Anna stiffened her spine. This big, overconfident and rude Yankee could go jump in the river. She wasn't about to hire him. She didn't need him or any other man. "I'm sorry, Mr. Cousins, but Bubba was wrong. I'm quite discriminating."

"I didn't mean to offend you." He smiled again. "I'm a builder by trade. I've done a lot of restoration and renovation work on the East Coast. In fact, I've worked on places older than this one. I suggest you give me a chance. You won't regret it."

Arrogant, Anna thought. Pushy. The last kind of man she wanted on Ashland. Yet, if he had the experience he said he did... She folded her arms across her chest. "Boston's a long way from Mississippi. May I ask what you're doing in Ames?"

He hesitated a moment, then slipped his hands into the front pockets of his blue jeans and shrugged. "Road trip. I'd never seen the South and the opportunity presented itself. So here I am."

He wasn't telling her everything. His answer had an awkward, almost rehearsed quality to it. As if it didn't fall off his tongue naturally. Anna searched his gaze, wondering what it was he'd kept hidden. And why.

He hiked his bag back onto his shoulder. "Forget it. You're obviously not interested, and there's always a job for someone with my qualifications." He descended the stairs and started for the magnolia grove. "See you around."

"Wait!"

He stopped and looked back at her, a grin tugging at the corners of his mouth. He knew he had her. Damn him.

"I'm only interested in summer help."

"By September, it'll be time for me to move on."

"I pay minimum wage."

"Room and board?"

"Room only. There's a kitchen in the guest quarters."

"Partial board. I expect cold drinks during the day, and the noon meal."

Anna narrowed her eyes. The man would endlessly irritate her. What she'd have liked to do was send him packing. But she needed his help, Ashland needed his help. If he had the credentials he promised, he would be a godsend.

She thought of the way he'd moved his hands over the chipped column. This was a man who had worked with his hands, a man who respected craftsmanship and the materials of building. She hadn't a doubt about that. And nobody else with any kind of restoration experience or skills was going to apply. She hadn't a doubt about that, either.

She needed him, and as dismayed as that made her, it was a fact. She drew in a deep breath and let it out on a huff. "You're hired, Mr. —"

"Rush," he corrected.

"Mr. Cousins," she repeated stiffly. "We'll start first thing in the morning. Come, I'll show you your quarters."

Without waiting for him, she started down the stairs and around to the rear of the house, dog at her side. Rush gazed after her, his eyes narrowed. Eighty-five degrees in the shade, and he had frostbite. Annabelle Ames had the lady-of-the-manor act down to a T. He should know—growing up he'd been dished a lot of that act. He didn't take that garbage anymore, not from anybody.

Yet her hand had been strong, Rush recalled, remembering the feel of it in his. Although small and delicately shaped, her skin had been tough from hard work. And her eyes... Rush cocked his head in thought. He'd caught a glimmer of something incredibly soft and uncertain in her eyes. Something that called to him on some sort of elemental, protective level.

Rush laughed to himself and descended the steps two at a time. The romantic atmosphere of this place was affecting him. Annabelle Ames was exactly what she seemed, nothing more and certainly nothing softer.

But that didn't mean he had to play by her rules. And he wasn't about to let some uppity Southern belle treat him like he was less than what he was. He was as good as anybody, and he made his own rules. Always.

He called it survival.

Rush caught up with her and matched his stride to hers. "Ms. Ames?" he asked, angling her an amused glance.

She looked at him. "Yes?"

"Are you going to call me Mr. Cousins all summer?" His question surprised her. He saw the emotion flit across her features before she had a chance to mask it. "Truthfully, Ms. Ames."

"Well, I..." She sucked in a quick breath and shook her head. "Probably not."

"So why don't we save ourselves the aggravation and drop the formality now?" He tucked his hands into the front pockets of his blue jeans and smiled. "How about it, boss?"

She smiled slowly, as if in spite of herself. The curving of her mouth softened her face, making her look younger, less...determined. In fact, Rush realized, she was attractive. Not technically pretty—her features were too strong for that. But there was a quiet beauty about her, a strength of character and feature, a quality that made her face different.

"All right," she answered slowly. "You may call me Anna."

Anna. It fit her in a way her full name didn't. It was strong and straightforward. No muss, no fuss. Rush smiled. "One more thing. Do you think you could tell that beast I'm okay? He's still looking at me as if he'd like to take a chunk out of my backside."

Anna laughed. Her soft, cultured drawl came out as an even softer, throatier, laugh and the sound played over his nerve endings, affecting him like a fine old wine. It was the kind of sound that made a man's mind wander, his pulse quicken. It had Rush wishing she would laugh again.

"You needn't worry," she said. "Blue won't attack you unless I give the command or you threaten me. He's very well trained."

"Well, that's a relief," Rush muttered wryly, eyeing the animal. "Remind me to get on your good side."

"If you're as experienced a builder as you say, you'll be on my good side."

"And if I'm not?"

"I'll sic Blue on you."

This time, it was he who laughed. "I think you mean that."

"Believe me, Mr. Cousins, I do."

They reached the building, a small, single-story frame structure with a wide front porch, and climbed the steps together. "This was the overseer's home," Anna murmured, opening the door, "back when Ashland was a working plantation. After the original structure burned in the forties, this one was built."

She crossed the threshold, and Rush followed her inside, his senses swimming with a sense of déjà vu so strong he couldn't speak. Anna seemed not to notice and continued to talk. "You'll find everything you need here. Linens in the closet over there." She pointed to her right. "The bedrooms are..."

At the back. There are two. Rush drew in a deep, steadying breath. He knew this floor plan; he recognized the light fixtures, the placement of windows, the brick fireplace.

"Use the first," she continued. "The other is smaller, like a..."

Nursery. Rush moved his gaze in that direction, wondering if he would feel this same overwhelming sense of recognition when he looked in that room for the first time. Wondering, too, if he wasn't losing his mind.

Anna moved toward the door. "The kitchen has a passable selection of cookware, dishes and the like.

Sorry, but there's no phone. If you need to make a call you can make arrangements with me. And if you need anything else, or have any questions, well . . . I'll be around."

He had questions, all right, questions about who he was and who had lived here years ago. Rush met her gaze, fighting to hold his impatience back. He was unaccustomed to waiting or inaction, and he liked neither. He forced an easy smile anyway. "It's a nice place. Who did you say used to live here?"

"The plantation manager and his wife. But Ashland hasn't been a working plantation in forty years." Anna expelled a frustrated-sounding breath. "Daddy leased and sold off the land, bit by bit, years ago."

Forty years. Two years after he was born. Rush flexed his fingers. "It's been empty that long?"

Anna gazed at him a moment before answering. "No. The overseer and his wife stayed. They rented the place for a while. Macy continued to keep house for us. Her husband found work in Greenville."

"They didn't have any children?"

She drew her eyebrows together, obviously surprised at the question. "They had a son. He died as an infant."

An infant? Or a young boy? Excitement coursed through Rush, and he had to work to keep it from showing. Could it be this easy? After a lifetime of wondering, could he have found his past so quickly and with so little effort?

"Why the interest?" she asked, gazing steadily at him.

He should have known she wouldn't keep her questions to herself. Even after only an hour with her, he knew that wasn't her way. Again, he forced a casual air. "This place has so much history, it almost begs for a story to be told." And there was one particular story he was interested in hearing. "Do you mind if I spend the day looking around the plantation?"

She hesitated, and her small smile disappeared. After a moment, she nodded. "Fine. But the interior of the house is off-limits."

He stiffened at her tone. "I hadn't planned to come traipsing through your home without invitation."

"I hadn't meant to imply that."

Like hell. He walked toward the door, anxious to get rid of her and look around. "If you don't mind, I'll have a phone installed. At my own expense, of course."

Again she hesitated, then inclined her head. "Fine. I don't have a problem with that."

"Good." He held the door open for her. "I'll see you at eight in the morning."

She followed him to the door and stepped out onto the porch. There, she looked over her shoulder at him. "Two more things. You'd better be as experienced as you say you are, or I won't think twice about firing you. And second, I sleep with Blue at my side and a gun under my pillow."

Rush stared at her a moment, narrowing his eyes. "I'll take that under advisement, Annabelle Ames."

She met his gaze evenly. "You do that, Rush Cousins."

Without another word, she turned and walked away. As she disappeared around the front corner of the house, he tipped his head back and laughed, reluctant admiration curling through him. Annabelle Ames was one tough lady. He might not enjoy working for her, but it certainly wouldn't be dull.

Chapter Two

The night shimmered with moisture. Fog had begun to roll off the river shortly after dark. It cloaked the grounds in diaphanous billows of white, reminding Anna of the nights she had sat in this very rocking chair, listening raptly to her father as he wove exciting, romantic tales about the Old South and their ancestors.

Anna smiled at the memory, listening now to the songs of the cricket and the bullfrog, being lulled by the rhythmic creak of her chair. The day had passed quickly and pleasurably. She had allowed herself the luxury of doing nothing productive. She'd picked flowers in what had once been the formal gardens, had walked to the levee and gazed for an hour at the lazy river; she'd sat under the largest magnolia on the plantation and read a book that had nothing to do with anything but enjoying herself. And now, she just sat, enjoying the richness of the white-black night.

She rested her head against the chair's high back. Her day would have been totally relaxing if not for Rush Cousins. No matter where she'd been on the plantation, she'd been aware of him, of his presence. That awareness had put her on edge, had made her feel vulnerable. He had violated her privacy in a way having other workers on Ashland's grounds in the past had not.

Rush Cousins took up a lot of space. He was the type of man who walked into a room and owned it. He had a kind of energy that dominated, that refused to be ignored.

Anna shuddered. It was going to be difficult for her to work with him. She wasn't comfortable with men like that, men who were big, confident and masculine. She didn't like being aware of her own femininity, or the vulnerability that came with it. She closed her eyes and an image from her fifteenth summer flashed lightninglike across the backs of her eyelids. An image of her sobbing and pushing at the boy's chest. Pushing as hard as she could but still being too small, too weak to free herself from his grasp.

Anna made a sound of fear and opened her eyes. Headlights cut across the darkness, illuminating both the fog and the landscape it concealed. She recognized her brother Lowell's car and sighed. Why had her brother chosen tonight to come see her? Why this moment, when she was suddenly feeling so vulnerable and uncertain?

At her feet, Blue whined. She reached down and stroked the dog's silky ears and head. "I know, boy. I feel the same way."

From the side of the house, she heard a car door slam, heard the murmur of male voices. Rush, she thought and wondered what he would think of her brother.

Lowell emerged out of the fog and started toward the gallery. The image of the Southern gentleman, Anna thought wryly. Tall, slim and blond, dressed in elegant evening clothes, he could have stepped out of the past, out of one of their father's romantic stories. How Lowell would laugh if he could read her thoughts.

He stopped at the base of the stairs and gazed unsmiling up at her. "Good evening, Annabelle," he said finally, softly.

"Lowell," she returned, forcing a light smile. "What brings you out here tonight?"

He climbed the stairs. "Ashland is my home. At least the last time I checked, I still owned half of this fabulous spread." He looked around him, his lips curling in distaste.

So, it was going to be one of those visits. A knot settled in Anna's chest, and she worked to breathe around it. "Of course you do. You just don't come around much."

"There's nothing here for me."

Hurt at his words speared through her. She tightened her fingers on the chair's arms. *"I'm* here, Lowell. Am I nothing to you?"

He held her gaze for a moment, then swung away from her and crossed to one of the huge columns. For long moments he stared out at the shrouded grounds.

Anna gazed at his stiff back, aching for the small, affectionate boy he had once been. Aching for the time when he had loved and needed her.

Tears stung her eyes, and she looked away. "Only June," she murmured, "and already so warm. It seems to get hotter every year."

Lowell glanced over his shoulder at her. "And you say that every year."

"I suppose I do."

Silence fell between them once more. Lowell took a pack of cigarettes from his shirt pocket, selected one and lit it. The match illuminated his face strangely, making his handsome features appear drawn and tight. And terribly unhappy.

Once again, Anna shifted her gaze. She didn't like seeing him this way. It hurt to see his unhappiness. "You met the new man," she said, needing to fill the silence. Her brother didn't respond, and she forged on. "He says he has building experience. In fact, he says he's done a lot of restoration work on the East Coast. If that's true, we should be able to—"

"Diversionary chitchat, Anna?"

She dropped her hands to her lap and laced her fingers together. "Just talking."

"Why? Isn't the quiet comfortable?"

She inched her chin up even as her palms began to sweat. He'd come spoiling for a fight. From experience she knew nothing she could say or do would dissuade him. She tried anyway. "You're my brother. Ashland is part yours. I thought you'd be interested."

"Half mine," he corrected. "And I'm not."

She stood and crossed to him. "What *are* you interested in, Lowell?" she asked. When he neither answered nor acknowledged her, she caught his arm. "Or aren't you interested in anything?"

He met her eyes then. In his she read an emotion akin to hatred. She caught her breath. "Lowell, what—"

"Selling this place," he said tightly. "That's what I'm interested in."

"No." Anna shook her head and took a step back. "No," she repeated. "Not ever."

"Half of it is mine."

"And half is mine." She flexed her fingers. While growing up she'd given in to him time and again. He'd been the baby, and she'd adored him. Not this time. She couldn't.

"I won't sell, Lowell."

He swore and swung away from her. He flicked his cigarette off the gallery; it landed with a hiss in the damp grass. When he turned back to her she saw by his expression that they'd just progressed from bitter words to a full-blown fight. "You're so hardheaded when it comes to this place. So blind."

"It's our home." She balled her hands into fists of frustration. "Our heritage. Why can't you see that?"

"It's a burden," he countered. "It's draining you, Anna. Look at yourself. Almost forty and dried up already."

The shot hit its mark, and she drew in a sharp breath. "Stop it, Lowell."

"Ashland's doing it to you, Anna. You have no life." This time it was she who swung away from him. He followed her, smelling her distress like blood, pressing his advantage. "When's the last time you had fun? When's the last time you went out—"

"That's where we're different," she shot back. "I don't have to go out partying every night to feel like I'm alive. I don't need expensive meals and clothes and cars to feel like I'm somebody. For me, Ashland is—''

"Everything?" He advanced on her, his eyes glittering with anger. With determination. "When's the last time you went out with a man, Annabelle?"

"I don't need—"

"Don't you long to be loved? To be held?" He stopped directly before her, and although she told herself to look away, she found she could not. "Don't you long to be a woman?"

Her eyes filled, and she whirled away from him. He knew what buttons to push, how to hurt her. Of course he did—he was her brother.

Again he followed her, but this time he didn't force her to look at him. Instead, he lightly stroked her hair. "Aren't you tired of being alone, Anna?"

Tears welled in her eyes. She blinked against them, but still they rolled down her cheeks. "If you would move back to Ashland, I wouldn't be."

"That's not what I meant, and you know it. I'm talking about a lover, a husband. A life partner, Annabelle. Not a brother." He rested his cheek against her hair. "If we sold Ashland, we could both start anew. We would be free."

She stiffened and jerked away from him. "Family shouldn't hurt each other, Lowell," she said softly. "They shouldn't prey on each other's emotions to get their way."

He laughed, the sound filled with bitterness. "It's an Ames tradition, my dear. Like so many others, handed down with pride."

"How can you say that?" Anna demanded, anger replacing hurt. "Mama—"

"Was a saint," Lowell muttered.

"She loved you. Doted on you, even."

"To make up for dear old Daddy. Isn't that right, Anna?" He arched his eyebrows, mocking her. "Mama, the long-suffering and saintly wife of Joshua Ames, the monster."

Anna opened her mouth to deny his words, to defend their father. But in many ways, he was just what Lowell had called him. "Mama did love you, Lowell. And her love had nothing to do with him. And Daddy... loved you, too. He just had difficulty—"

"Being anything but cruel?" Lowell raked a hand through his light hair, so like hers. "You're hopeless. You always have been. You seclude yourself out here, living in the past and in those ridiculous stories Daddy told you. No wonder no man ever comes around. What would a real, flesh-and-blood male want with an unfeeling martyr like you? You're going to be alone forever, Anna. Or until you let go of this place and learn to live in the real world."

His words cut her, so deeply it burned. She drew in a shuddering breath, tears closing around her throat. "What's happened to you?" she whispered. "You didn't always play so dirty."

"I wasn't so desperate before."

Desperate. That word again. How she despised it. How helpless and trapped it made her feel. Unwittingly, she thought of the new strands of gray hair she'd spotted just that morning. Soon her hair would be more gray than blond. Time was making its mark on her, as well as Ashland.

Forty. She fought the sense of panic that suddenly squeezed against her chest. Past her childbearing years. Past the age when men pursued. Not that they ever had in the first place.

Alone. She would end up alone.

Anna stiffened her spine. She liked the gray. And she liked her life. She was fine. Happy. She didn't need a man in her life, and although she would have loved to be a mother, she had her first-graders. She would live without knowing that experience.

She would not allow her brother the power to make her start doubting herself. "Go away, Lowell," she said wearily. "You've hurt me enough for tonight."

Anna turned and started into the house, knowing that if Lowell followed her, she couldn't stop him. As he'd said, he owned half of Ashland.

"Annabelle..."

She looked back and for one brief moment she thought she saw a glimmer of the boy he had once been. Then the softness vanished, replaced once more with bitterness and cynicism. Without waiting to see what he'd wanted, she retreated to the solace of Ashland.

The next morning, Rush carried a cup of coffee out onto his small front porch. The day was clear and bright, the sky a cloudless blue. Although not even seven, according to the thermostat outside his kitchen window, the temperature had already hit the eighty-degree mark.

It felt it, Rush thought, absently scratching his bare chest. And it felt good. The heat. Being here. Standing half naked on this front porch and watching the day rise over Ashland.

Did it feel so right because he'd been a young boy at Ashland? Was he responding to this place because he recognized it, or because he wanted to?

Rush turned his gaze to the grove of magnolias and took a sip of his coffee, enjoying its strong, almost-bitter taste. He didn't know. He'd spent the day before combing the plantation grounds, searching for something that would trigger the same response in him that the music box had.

This house had come the closest, yet when he'd logically examined his recognition of the floor plan, he'd had to admit that it wasn't an unusual one. In fact, it was standard. In his years of building he'd worked on similar houses.

So he'd vacillated between being certain he'd visited Ashland Plantation in the past and being certain he was going through some sort of ridiculous mid-life crisis.

He made a sound of frustration. He wasn't accustomed to uncertainty. Since he'd been old enough to take charge of his life, he had. He'd always known exactly what he wanted and what he felt, and he'd acted accordingly. Even those months he'd lived on the streets, he'd been certain of his every action and of how he would survive.

Rush frowned and brought the cup to his lips once more. Frustrating, too, had been his inability to put Annabelle Ames from his mind. He'd caught himself thinking of her, remembering something she'd said or the way she'd looked at him. Several times during the course of the day he'd caught a glimpse of her, and each time he'd given her a wide berth. Because she'd wanted to be alone, and because he had, too.

She'd been up as late as he the night before. He'd seen her lights burning long after her brother had left.

Lowell Ames. Rush's frown deepened, remembering his meeting with the other man the night before. They'd come face-to-face in the driveway as Lowell had alighted from his vehicle. Rush had detested the man on sight—even before he'd heard how he treated his sister.

Anna's and Lowell's voices had carried on the fog, and he had listened to their argument. Listened shamelessly. He would use every opportunity to try to unearth a clue to his past, would even stoop to eaves-dropping.

And he'd learned much about the brother and sister, Rush thought, turning his gaze to Ashland's huge square columns. He narrowed his eyes. Where Anna was strong, Lowell was weak and self-pitying. Where Anna had character, Lowell had attitude. Anna would do whatever was necessary to save Ashland; Lowell had no love for the plantation at all—in fact he wished they could be rid of it.

Rush took a long swallow of the coffee. He could understand Annabelle's love of this place. He found Ashland beautiful, even with her cracks and crum-bling plaster, her overgrown gardens, her hue of age and decay. How could Lowell Ames, having grown up here, not love it also? And how had the brother and sister turned out so differently?

He moved his gaze across the deep first-floor gal-lery and row of floor-to-ceiling windows beyond. He was curious about this house, this family, its history. He wondered where—and if—he fit into the puzzle.

And he wondered about Annabelle.

He'd never met a woman quite like her before, and she fascinated him. He sensed in her a real strength of character. Of purpose, certainly. She had guts, verve. She could hold her own with anyone.

He smiled, remembering her final words to him yes-terday, laughing softly. *"I sleep with Blue at my side and a gun under my pillow.''* He had no doubt she wouldn't hesitate to use either to protect herself. Or Ashland.

He shook his head. She infuriated him. Her cool superiority grated on his nerves, conjuring memories from his youth, ones he preferred stayed in the past.

What made her tick? he wondered, downing the last of his coffee. He had no use for games or false modesty. Since he'd been old enough to notice, females had been interested. They usually sent him signals: the fluttering of lashes, sidelong glances or suggestive chitchat. He'd had none of those from Annabelle. She didn't want to be his friend. Or anything else.

Which suited him just fine. He'd come to Ashland for one reason only, and it wasn't a fling with a Southern belle with a superiority complex.

Rush lifted his gaze to the second-floor gallery. As if his thoughts had materialized her, Annabelle stood at the edge of the railing looking out at the new day. She wore a lightweight robe, cinched at the waist. Her feet were bare, her hair sleep-tousled.

As he watched, the breeze caught the fabric, molding it to her hips and thighs, outlining her slender body. His blood stirred, and Rush told himself to go inside and give her the privacy she thought she had.

He didn't move a muscle.

She looked down. Their eyes met. The day seemed suddenly heavy and still, the air electric with possibilities. She looked soft in that white robe, with the sunlight playing over her and her blond hair tumbling over her shoulder. Softer than he'd thought she could be.

And womanly; lush and inviting.

Rush sucked in a sharp breath as arousal speared through him. He imagined going to her, peeling away that white cotton robe to reveal skin whiter, softer, than the fabric. But warm with excitement. And later, damp from his mouth and tongue.

The power of the image, of his arousal, shocked him. This was no mild stirring of the blood, no simple instance of attraction or appreciation. That what he felt was a reaction to this particular woman shocked him more.

Rush fought back the image, and his arousal. It wouldn't do, not at all. A tryst between them would complicate things, would muddy his thinking, his sense of purpose. Besides, Annabelle Ames was not the type of woman who dallied. He wasn't even sure whether blood or ice ran through her veins.

Remembering the haughty way she had lifted her chin and looked at him, he decided on ice. Rush lifted his coffee mug in a silent and impersonal salute, then turned and went inside to take a cold shower.

Anna watched Rush disappear inside his house, her knees buckling beneath her. She grabbed the gallery railing for support and drew in a shuddering breath. Dear Lord, what had happened to her?

Her cheeks burned as she thought of the way her body had responded to him. Her nipples had become erect; her sex, shamelessly wet. She'd had to fight to breathe; she was still fighting. And even though she'd ordered herself to retreat from the gallery and his scrutiny, she'd been unable to move.

She, the woman who had been called unresponsive and cold even by the man she'd been engaged to marry, had felt like a mare in heat.

Anna pictured Rush as he had been moments before, the sun spilling over his broad, muscular chest, his eyes heavy-lidded with sleep. Her pulse stirred and she clenched her hands into fists. Would it be different with this man, she wondered, her cheeks growing hot with color? If he put his hands on her, would she melt? Or freeze?

Her heart began to thrum against the wall of her chest, her palms to sweat. She recognized the sensations, so different from the ones of moments ago. Fear. Of being touched. Of being proved a failure again.

Frigid.

Anna tried to push the word, the description, away, but it lingered, gnawing at her. She'd been called that more than once, by more than one man. The first time, she'd been fifteen; the last, she'd been thirty-five. It didn't hurt any less now than then.

Anna gazed at Rush's empty porch, her chest tight. He'd felt nothing. Obviously. She thought of the way he'd lifted his cup, then jauntily turned and walked away, and she made a sound of pain and self-derision. What was he supposed to have done? Acted like some lovesick Romeo? Read her poetry from below? Or even more ludicrous, overcome with passion, charged through Ashland's front doors to ravish her?

She leaned against one of the columns, her heart and breath slowing. This was crazy. Ridiculous. Why had she responded so forcefully to this man? A stranger?

Anna shook her head, stunned. She wasn't the type to swoon. She wasn't…a physical woman. Not in that way, anyway. And even if she hadn't been told how cold she was so many times, she couldn't deny the wall of ice that went up every time a man tried to touch her.

"Don't you want to be loved, Anna? Don't you want to be held? Cherished?" Lowell's hurtful words from the previous night played through her brain, and as

they had then, tears stung her eyes. She squeezed them shut. She did want to be loved. She *was* lonely. Dammit, she wished she could deny it, but she couldn't.

Just as she wished she could deny her brother's other words. *"No wonder no man ever comes around. What would a real, flesh-and-blood male want with a cold, unfeeling martyr like you? You're going to end up alone, Anna."*

She brushed the tears from her cheeks, impatient with herself, cursing Lowell for knowing her vulnerabilities, knowing the places and ways he could get to her.

But she wouldn't sell Ashland, no matter what he said or did, no matter how deeply he hurt her.

Anna pushed away from the column. She hadn't cried last night—she hadn't slept but at least she'd kept her emotions in check. Now, the tears welled against the backs of her eyes, in her chest and throat. She fought them back. She had to be strong; she couldn't fall back on traditional feminine behavior. For if she fell, there would be no one there to catch her. She'd learned that long ago.

What happened this morning had been a fluke, some sort of a delayed reaction to her fight with Lowell. She drew in a deep, calming breath. She was on edge and feeling the effects of a night with little sleep.

Sure, she told herself. When she came face-to-face with Rush later, she would feel nothing but impatience to get started, and hope that he had the building experience he'd promised. She drew in another breath. And in a couple of days, the sting of her brother's words would have subsided, and she would be able to think of Lowell—and her life—without wanting to cry.

Until then, she would do the best she could. After all, what other choice did she have? Taking one last glance at the overseer's house and its empty front porch, she turned and went inside to dress.

An hour later, Anna emerged from Ashland, bathed and dressed, her protective armor firmly around her. Rush sat on the gallery, waiting for her in the same rocking chair she'd occupied the night before. He wore faded denims, a cream-colored polo shirt and well-worn deck shoes; he'd shaved and brushed and completely eliminated the cobwebs of sleep. But she took one look at him and pictured him as he'd been earlier that morning: half naked, his furred chest bronze from the sun, muscular from work; his stomach, hard and flat, dusted with hair that disappeared in a V beneath the partially fastened waistband of his jeans.

Anna swallowed, her mouth suddenly desert-dry. His feet had been bare, his eyes still lazy with sleep, his hair mussed as if from a lover's fingers. He'd appeared every inch the self-confident male animal and had made her feel every inch the swooning female.

He still did. Dammit.

Anna stiffened and clutched her clipboard to her chest. He'd toppled her barriers without even trying.

She wasn't the only one. Blue lay at Rush's feet, his big head lying across Rush's shoes. The dog didn't even glance her way. Some guard dog, she thought. Great protection.

Rush caught sight of her and smiled. After extricating himself from the adoring Blue, he crossed to her. He stopped before her, so close she saw the gold flecks in his hazel eyes and caught the clean, soapy scent of his morning shower. "Pretty day," he murmured.

There was something intimate in his eyes, his voice. As if their relationship had somehow deepened. The thought scared her witless. She worked to keep her turmoil from showing, curling her fingers tighter around the clipboard. "Yes, it is." She cleared her throat. "Are you ready to begin?"

She sounded like the spinster schoolteacher she was, Anna thought. Prim and old-fashioned.

Dried up, Lowell had called her.

"If I wasn't, I'd still be in bed."

His words brought an image to mind, one of him and her and a big, soft bed.

As if he read her thoughts, Rush's smile deepened, and he swept his gaze warmly over her. "I see you're ready to get started, too. But I have to say, I liked the robe more."

Anna looked down at herself, at the ancient, baggy trousers, the sexless T-shirt and men's work boots, and heat rushed over her in a debilitating wave. Her clothes were practical. Just like she was. Sturdy, plain and practical. She'd defiantly chosen them for comfort, and because they were about as feminine as a tree trunk.

Anna stiffened her spine, angry at him for the intimate reference; at herself for allowing him to get to her. "First of all, I'm here to work, Mr. Cousins. Not to lounge. Secondly, I think we need to get something straight. I didn't appreciate that little scene this morning. And I expect it not to happen again."

"Excuse me...*Anna.*" He placed his fists on his hips. "I must have missed something here. Exactly what *scene* are you referring to?"

She felt color climb her cheeks, and silently swore. "This morning. On the galler—"

"When you were peeping at me, you mean."

"What!"

"That's the way it seemed to me."

"I certainly was not *peeping* at you. I happen to see it the other way."

"Odd that you should. You knew where I was staying, but I had no idea where your bedroom was." He arched his eyebrows arrogantly, every inch the supremely confident male. "And I had a lot fewer clothes on than you did."

Blue thumped his tail on the gallery floor, as if agreeing with Rush. Anna shot the dog a dirty look. It didn't help that Rush was right, damn him. She tossed her head back. "Fine. I won't use that section of gallery in the morning."

"Oh, please . . ." He gestured broadly with his right hand. "Go ahead. Your being there didn't bother me in the least."

But it had bothered her plenty. Even now she could recall how she had felt during those few moments. She gritted her teeth. "I'm glad to hear that. I wouldn't want to have intruded on *your* privacy."

He smiled. "I appreciate the sentiment, Annabelle. And the apology."

Apology? "Of all the arrogant, insufferable—" Anna bit back the string of angry expletives and swung away from him. She would not let him get to her; she simply would not. "I thought we'd begin with the exterior of the house, then move inside. I'd like your opinion on—"

"Don't you ever admit you're wrong?"

She looked over her shoulder and met his gaze. "You're being a bit presumptuous, don't you think?"

"You mean, for the hired help."

She lifted her chin. "Yes."

"But you need me more than I need you. And we both know it."

Anger, white-hot and barely leashed, flashed through her. "That remains to be seen, doesn't it? Right now, all I have is your word to go on. The word of an out-of-work drifter."

A muscle worked in his jaw. His eyes burned with temper. Gone was the image of the sexy rascal, the charming rake. This man could be dangerous if pushed too far. And that was exactly what she'd done.

She took a step back, wondering if Blue would come to her aid, should she need him. From the corner of her eye she saw that he was sleeping, and decided that she was on her own.

Rush closed the distance between them. "I'm not a liar, Anna," he said softly, the words edged with steel. "Don't ever again imply that I am." He held out his hand, visibly fighting for control. "Give me that blasted clipboard, and I'll get started. I'm on the clock, here."

She looked at his outstretched hand, then met his gaze once more. "You're not starting without me. I'm going to be working right alongside you." She arched her eyebrows haughtily. "You have a problem with that?"

He made a sound of frustration. "Damn right, I do. This type of work is best left to a professional. You'll slow me down and get one of us hurt."

"By professionals, you mean men."

"In this case, yes."

She squared her shoulders. "You, sir, are a chauvinist. I'll have you know, I've been making repairs on Ashland since I was old enough to take orders."

"But this year," he said smoothly, "you have me. So, why don't you just—"

"Relax and enjoy it? Sit back and do some needlework?" She gave her head an angry shake. "I don't think so."

"Well, look at you. A good-size wind would blow you away." He laughed at her outrage. "Besides, what's wrong with needlework?"

"I can assure you, I have withstood much more than a *good-size wind*. And I abhor needlework." She narrowed her eyes in challenge. "My place, my money. My call, Cousins."

"Fine." He threw up his hands. "Tag along. But you'll only slow me down."

"I'm going to enjoy proving you wrong," she muttered. "I'm going to enjoy it a lot."

Chapter Three

It irritated the hell out of him, but Anna did prove him wrong. Rush shifted his gaze to where she worked, a few feet to his left. A hundred-plus degrees on Ashland's slate roof, her T-shirt drenched with sweat, her cheeks pink with exertion, and she continued to hammer the pieces of slate in place without murmur or complaint.

Over the last few days she'd worked alongside him, worked until he was sure her muscles must be trembling with fatigue. Yet she'd never complained. She'd never demurred over a job he asked her to do. And she most certainly hadn't slowed him down.

But she had driven him crazy. When she pulled out the high-and-mighty routine, he saw red. He'd encountered more than his share of holier-than-thou's growing up, and he wasn't about to put up with it now.

And so he'd pushed at her, pushed until she, too, saw red.

And in the process he'd discovered something interesting about Ms. Annabelle Ames. When she was angry, she forgot to be cool. Or haughty. Or stiff. She came alive with heat, with passion.

That woman stirred his blood and his senses. She made him think about making love, had him wondering how she would move beneath him, if she would cry out his name, if she would lead or be led.

Even as he acknowledged the lunacy of his thoughts, his body responded to them. Rush muttered an oath. This was crazy. He wasn't an untried boy; she was neither overtly sexual nor traditionally beautiful. He wasn't interested in her. She wasn't interested in him. Hell, they could barely tolerate each other's company. And yet ...

Anna paused in her hammering to wipe the sweat from her brow; as she did, the damp clingy fabric of her shirt cupped and outlined one breast. Rush gazed at the swell of cloth over flesh, awareness balling in the pit of his stomach.

He swallowed, picturing her as she'd been that morning on the gallery, remembering his arousal. Wondering again what it would be like between them.

Rush shook his head and dragged his gaze away. He picked up his drill and flipped it on. He needed to be smart. He needed to earn her trust, needed her to open up to him so he could question her. To do that he had to keep his wits about him. He couldn't be thinking about soft, warm skin or eyes the color of lapis.

Rush frowned, forcing his thoughts back to his reason for coming to Ashland. He was no closer to knowing who he was than the day he'd arrived. He needed

Anna to open up, needed her willing to answer questions. He looked at her once more, frustration welling in his chest. She rarely let down her guard, he'd never seen her relaxed. And not once had she talked about herself or her family. The questions he'd asked as she'd shown him through the nearly empty house had been met with icy reserve.

And yet he'd caught her looking at him from the corner of her eye, had sensed a curiosity, an interest, that went beyond casual.

Rush made a sound of self-derision and frustration. Right. That's why she jumped if his hand or arm happened to brush against her. That's why she kept an arm's-length distance between them at all times.

"Dammit!" Anna dropped her hammer and grabbed her thumb.

"You okay?"

She yanked off her work glove and brought her thumb to her mouth, her eyes watering. "Fine."

"Let me take a look." He squatted down beside her, and drew her hand away from her mouth. Already her nail was turning blue. After removing his gloves, he ran his fingers gently over hers. "It looks bad. Better put some ice on it."

She jerked her hand away, her cheeks bright with color. "I told you, it's fine."

He sat back on his haunches. "I don't believe I've ever met a more stubborn woman."

She glared at him. "Down here it's considered bad manners to be so pushy."

He laughed. "I'll take that under advisement."

"I'll bet." She stuck her thumb back in her mouth and lowered her gaze to the roof. "Dammit," she said again, this time around her finger. "I broke the slate."

He clucked his tongue. "Don't worry about it, Anna. It happens to the best of us. Even those who aren't so clumsy."

"I'm not clumsy," she snapped. "I just slipped and—"

"Smashed your thumb and a piece of slate to smithereens." He shook his head, biting back laughter. "You're right. How could I call *you* clumsy?"

"If you hadn't been staring at me..." She bit the words back, flushing.

Rush smiled, pleased that she'd been aware of his scrutiny. And he liked the way she puffed up with annoyance, like an outraged bird. "Watching me, were you?"

"Certainly not! Just aware..." She caught herself again and arched her eyebrows in mock outrage. "You, sir, are no gentleman."

"Never claimed to be."

"Of course not." She slipped her glove back on and picked up her hammer, as a shudder of fatigue moved across her features.

Rush touched her arm. "You're tired, Anna. Why don't we break for—"

"I don't need to break." She shook off his hand. "And seeing as you're on the clock, I suggest you get back at it, too."

"Nope. It's after twelve. It's bloody hot, and I'm tired." He started toward the ladder. "If you want to stay up here and fry, fine. I'm going to get lunch."

Without waiting for her to argue, he descended the ladder and started for the house. Anna watched him go, the desire to follow him warring with pride. Arrogant, she fumed as fatigue won out over pride, and she scooted toward the ladder. He was rude and overconfident. She didn't like him, she decided. And she certainly wasn't attracted to him.

You, Anna, are a liar.

Anna gritted her teeth. She couldn't keep her eyes off him. While they worked, she'd found herself watching him: his eyes as he studied the building, his hands as he inspected a crack or break. She found herself waiting, almost breathlessly, for him to look at her, to speak to her.

As she waited breathlessly for the response both evoked in her—the warm spot at the apex of her thighs that spread until her entire body felt lit by a hidden flame, the trembling sensation in her limbs, the fluttering of her pulse points.

Anna squeezed her eyes shut and drew in a deep breath. He scared her witless. Because he had the ability to break through all her defenses, leaving her exposed and weak. Because he made her want something that had always been just beyond her reach.

This was insanity, she told herself, opening her eyes, firming her resolve. She could overcome her feelings. Or ignore them. She'd overcome much tougher obstacles in her life.

She pulled off her work gloves, tossed them aside and quickly descended the ladder. She found him waiting for her on the front gallery. Ignoring his smug expression, she lifted her chin and moved regally past him to the front door. He followed her, and without speaking they crossed through Ashland's cavernous interior to the kitchen. Modernized in the space-age-loving late fifties and early sixties, the kitchen was an anachronism in the Civil War-era house.

"I'll make some sandwiches."

"No, you'll sit with an ice pack and *I'll* make sandwiches." She opened her mouth to protest, and he glared at her. "You're hurt, you're exhausted, and I may not be a gentleman, but I'm not a total cad, either."

"I don't need—"

"Sit," he ordered, yanking out one of the vinyl-and-chrome chairs.

She disliked being ordered about in her own home, but the thought of just sitting and doing nothing, even if only for a minute or two, was too inviting. She sank onto the chair, an involuntary sigh of pleasure slipping past her lips.

"Good girl," he said, going to the freezer for ice. Within moments he'd put together an ice pack and handed it to her.

Her thumb throbbed. Anna held the ice to it, wincing at the pressure. She leaned her head against the chair back and shut her eyes, waiting for the ice to numb the pain.

"Know what your problem is?" Rush asked conversationally, laying out eight slices of bread.

"Tell me," she answered dryly, not bothering to open her eyes. "I can hardly wait."

"You're afraid to let go and be a human."

"A woman, you mean."

"No, I didn't mean that." He slathered the bread with mayonnaise. "But what's wrong with being a woman?"

She peered at him from half-lifted lids. "Nothing. I like being a woman." He turned back to the sandwiches, laying a slab of ham on each. "There're some carrot and celery sticks in the fridge," she said, her voice wobbling with fatigue.

He made a face. "Any chips?"

"Sorry." She watched as he piled the sandwiches on a plate and set it on the table, then went to the refrigerator for the pitcher of iced tea.

"It's okay to be weak sometimes," he said softly, taking the seat across from hers. "To be frightened. It's part of being alive."

A shudder ran through her, and she shook her head and met his eyes. "Not from where I'm sitting."

He held her gaze a moment, his own inscrutable. Then he selected a sandwich and began to eat. "How long has Ashland been your responsibility?"

"Totally mine for just over ten years. Since Daddy died. Before that..." Anna shook her head. "Never mind."

"Before that, what?"

She selected a carrot stick, toyed with it for a moment, then tossed it down, untasted. "After Mama died, Daddy needed a lot of help with Ashland. I was the natural choice."

He took another bite, chewing thoughtfully. "And you didn't expect that?"

"No. I...I thought he had everything under control. I thought he ran things. But it was always Mama. Even when we were young. So when she died—"

"The load shifted to you."

"Yes."

"No other family members around to help out?"

Lowell. Their argument came crashing back, with it a biting sense of betrayal. Anna tensed and met Rush's eyes. "You met my brother Lowell the other night. And I'm sure, after having spent a week in Ames, you know a fair bit about him. Including the fact that he has no interest in Ashland."

"I do know that," Rush said, toying with a tea-spoon. "I was referring to other relations. Aunts, uncles, cousins. Surely you and your brother aren't the last of the Ameses."

"But we are. Mama was the only child of only children. Daddy lost one brother when he was in his teens, the other before he and his wife had children."

Rush frowned. "No cousins at all? It's hard to believe."

Anna arched her eyebrows. "You must be one of those people with an army of relations."

"Actually," Rush said quietly, "I have no one."

No one. Something in the way he said the words, the look in his eyes as he'd said them, plucked at her heartstrings. She lifted her eyebrows in feigned outrage. "Mr. Cousins, I find your curiosity most untoward."

Rush laughed. "Untoward? I didn't think people talked like that anymore."

She laughed. "Down here we do."

"That's right. All that highfalutin language and manners."

"And all that Yankee care-be-damned brashness."

"Yankee?" Rush leaned toward her, amused. "Honey, didn't anybody tell you, that war ended years ago."

"Not down here." She smiled and fluttered her lashes. "I was ten before I realized that *damn* and *Yankee* were two words."

He tipped his head back and laughed. "You all don't say?"

She patted her mouth with a napkin. "It's *y'all.* And I do say."

For a moment their eyes held, the silence between them heavy with awareness. As if uncomfortable, he caught her hand and inspected her thumb with exaggerated seriousness. After a moment, he lifted his eyes to hers. "You'll live."

She swallowed. "I told you."

"That you did."

Instead of releasing her hand, he continued to hold it in his, moving his fingers over the delicate ridges of her knuckles, studying, exploring. Her pulse fluttered and heat moved languorously over her. She told herself to draw her hand away from his; she hadn't the strength of will. She hadn't the desire.

He laced their fingers, meeting her gaze once more. How had this happened? she wondered, suddenly breathless. How had they gone from combatant to companionable? Companionable to... this? And at what point had she let down her guard and allowed him in?

She didn't know. At this moment, she didn't even care. The heat was enough, slow and sweet and sanity-stealing. It flowed over her until she felt certain she must glow with it.

He brought his free hand to her cheek. She made a small, involuntary sound of pleasure, and tipped her face into the caress. "Do you ever think about giving up, Anna?" he asked suddenly, his voice soft and thick. "Of selling Ashland and running away?"

For long moments she stared at their joined hands, then looked back at him. "No," she whispered. "Never. I couldn't."

He tightened his fingers; he lowered his head. Anticipation trembled through her, fear on its heels. They warred within her until anticipation won. She parted her lips.

"Anna? Anybody home? It's me, Travis."

Anna jumped guiltily, yanking free of Rush's grasp. She looked from Rush to the kitchen doorway, reality and reason reasserting themselves. Dear God, what had she been about to do?

"In the kitchen, Trav," she called, running a trembling hand through her hair. "Come on back."

A moment later Travis appeared in the kitchen doorway. Dressed in an expensive business suit, a gold watch gleaming at his wrist, and his thick, dark hair graying at the temples, he presented the picture of financial success. When he caught sight of Rush, his smile faltered. For a moment he gazed silently at Rush, then turned back to her.

"I was hoping you could break to go to lunch with me," he said quietly. "I see I'm too late."

Anna flushed, even as she told herself she had nothing to feel guilty about. Standing, she crossed to him. "I'm so sorry, Travis. If I'd known, I would have waited."

She kissed his cheek, then slipped her arm through his and drew him into the kitchen. "Sit. I'll make you a sandwich."

"No. You're an angel for offering, though." He squeezed her hand. When she winced, he looked at her in concern. "What's happened?"

"It's nothing." She pulled her hands from his, aware of Rush's amused gaze upon them. "A silly accident with a hammer."

"Let me see." Travis caught her hand gently, his expression the picture of worry. "It looks pretty nasty. Maybe you should see a doctor. I could call—"

"Nonsense," Anna said crisply. "You're as bad as Rush."

"Rush?" Travis repeated, turning his gaze to where Rush sat.

Rush smiled and saluted. "That's me."

Anna made the introductions. "This is Travis Gentry, an old friend."

"I see that," Rush said, arching an eyebrow, deliberately looking at their still-joined hands.

Anna flushed and drew her hand out of Travis's. "Rush is working for me this summer."

"That's right," Travis said. "Anna's... handyman."

Rush inclined his head. "Yeah, Anna's handy... man."

Travis frowned slightly, moving his gaze from Rush to Anna and back. If Anna didn't know Travis better, she would have thought he looked uncertain. "Where'd you say you're from?"

"I didn't." Lifting his lips in a slow, satisfied smile, Rush pushed his chair back from the table and stood. "I'd better get back to work. See you on the roof, Anna."

Anna watched Rush walk away, a soft breath shuddering past her lips. What had gone on just now? She had the feeling that left to their own primitive instincts, the two men would have been at each other's throats.

"Anna?"

She jerked her gaze back to Travis's. His eyes upon hers were openly curious. And too observant. She shook her head and smiled. "I'm sorry. I'm a little tired. What did you say?"

"I asked where the man's from."

"Boston," she murmured. "He's done a good bit of restoration work up there."

"You don't say," Travis murmured, sounding anything but convinced.

"I can't believe my good fortune."

"Hmm." Travis drew his eyebrows together. "Annabelle, honey, are you sure it's safe letting that man into the house?"

"Rush? Of course. Why?"

"What do you really know about him? He's a drifter."

Annoyed, she moved away from her old friend, crossing to the sink. "That doesn't mean he's a criminal, Travis."

"But it does say something about his character." He closed the distance between them once more. "I worry about you being out here, all alone."

"I have Blue." Anna smiled. "And that snub-nosed .38 you insisted I have. What more protection do I need?"

"A man living here with you."

"I'll run an ad," she teased. "Come on, Trav, I'm fine. Let's drop it, okay?"

He did, but reluctantly, she could tell. "I just don't want anything to happen to you."

She smiled. "I know. You're a good friend. Now, have a seat and tell me what brings you out here today. Something more than lunch, I'll bet." She poured him an iced tea, then refilled her own glass and sat across from him. "Did you finally propose to the widow Grace? Or did she dump you for taking too long?"

"I came because of Lowell."

Anna's heart sank. Travis must have seen it on her face because he murmured, "I'm sorry."

She took a deep breath. "What happened?"

"He came to me for money again."

"Oh." She trailed her finger around the rim of her glass. "How much?"

Travis hesitated. "A lot."

"I'm a big girl, Trav. I can take it. How much?"

"Ten thousand."

"Oh, my God." Anna stood and crossed to the sink and the window above it. *Ten thousand dollars.* Her salary wasn't much more than that, yet Lowell wanted Travis to just . . . give it to him.

She brought a hand to her forehead and rubbed at the tightness there. Why did Lowell need that much money? What would he do with it?

She turned back to Travis. "Did you give it to him?"

Again Travis hesitated, then he shook his head and met her eyes. "Not this time. I hope you don't think less of me, or that I'm not his friend—"

She shook her head. "I would never think that."

"It wasn't the money, Anna. I have plenty of that. It's Lowell. I'm worried about him. He's out of control. He's . . ." Travis made a sound of frustration and dragged a hand through his dark hair. "I don't know what his problems are. But it . . . hurts to see him this way."

They had all been close growing up. Like siblings. Travis and Lowell had been inseparable, although by the end of high school they had drifted apart. By that age, the differences in the men they would become had already become apparent. Travis had drive and ambition, a fire in his belly to succeed; Lowell had nothing but anger and bitterness. Those differences had driven the two apart.

Anna sighed. "He's after me to sell Ashland."

"Again?"

"Worse than ever. He..." Anna lowered her eyes. "He said some ... cruel things. Ugly things."

"What did you tell him?"

"I told him no. That I'd never sell Ashland." Anna met her old friend's eyes. "Maybe I'm being selfish. Maybe I—"

"Hell no, you're not. Don't even think it. It's Lowell who has the problem, not you."

"So, what do I do?"

"How can I tell you that when I'm wrestling with that same question myself?" Travis made a sound of frustration. "But I don't think giving him money is the answer. I never should have in the first place."

Although they never spoke of it, Anna knew that over the years Travis had lent Lowell thousands of dollars. Ironic that growing up Travis had been the poor one, and they the rich Ameses. Now Travis was one of the richest men in the state. And she and Lowell had nothing. Except Ashland.

"You've already done too much for us," she murmured.

Travis turned to her, his eyes hot with an emotion Anna didn't recognize. "You've never asked me for anything, Anna."

"Your friendship is all I've ever wanted from you. It means more to me than you could know."

"I'd help you in any way I could. I'd give you... anything you asked for."

"I know, Travis. I do." Suddenly uncomfortable, she swung back to the window and the bright day beyond.

A little brown sparrow sat on the roof of the bird-house, chest and feathers puffed out, as if protecting her home.

"I offered him a job."

Anna turned. "What?"

"Lowell. I offered him a position. Actually, the choice from a number of them with my various holdings. To my way of thinking, that's what he needs."

She drew in a deep breath, hope blooming inside her. "What did he say?"

"I'm sorry." Travis lifted his hands in a gesture of futility. "He said no."

Anna let out her breath, disappointment hitting her with the force of a blow to her chest. "You're right, he needs to work. He needs a purpose in his life." Tears welled in her eyes, clogged her throat. "I don't know what to do, Travis. I don't know how to reach him. Every time I try, he lashes out at me."

Travis stood and crossed to her. He held her to his chest and stroked her hair. "I know. I wish I had the answer."

She tipped her head back and met his eyes. "This isn't even your problem."

Sadness moved over his features, and Anna was reminded again of their childhood together. Sometimes Travis had looked exactly this way, sad and so lost. As it had then, his sadness twisted at her heartstrings.

Standing on tiptoe, she kissed his cheek. "You're such a dear. I don't know what I would do without you."

He opened his mouth, then, as if changing his mind about what he wanted to say, cleared his throat. "I need to get back to the office."

She smiled and stepped out of his arms. "And my roof's waiting."

They took the back door, descended the stairs and walked toward his car in silence. When they reached it, Travis stopped, frowning. "Be careful, Anna. I don't want to see you hurt."

"Lowell's my brother. He wouldn't—"

"I wasn't talking about Lowell." He lifted his gaze to the roof and Anna followed it. Rush crouched on the edge of the roof, looking down at them. She felt rather than saw the intensity of his gaze, and a shiver moved over her, a sensation that had nothing to do with fear.

"You don't have to worry," she murmured. "I'll be fine."

"You're a big girl, right?"

She smiled. "Right."

Travis touched her cheek lightly, then opened the car door and slid inside. "Let's go out to dinner. Soon."

"I'd like that."

He started to close the door, then stopped and met her eyes again. "If you want me to give Lowell the money, Anna, I will."

Tears sprang to her eyes; once more, she fought them off. "No. He needs..." She shook her head. "No, Travis. But thanks. I appreciate your concern."

He opened his mouth as if to say something else, then shook his head. Lifting his hand in goodbye, he started the car and drove off. Anna watched until he disappeared from sight, a strange sensation balling in her chest, at once bittersweet and sad, and yearning.

Something had been on Travis's mind—something other than Lowell's troubles. She'd had the sense that Travis wasn't happy, that he needed something from her she wasn't able to give him.

She frowned. Travis was the most self-assured man she knew. Everything he'd ever wanted, he'd gotten. But today—

"Touching reunion," Rush said from behind her. "I was moved."

Anna whirled around, startled. "I didn't know you were standing there."

"Obviously." He dropped a broken drill bit into his pocket. "Did you and your little friend have a nice visit?"

Little friend? She stiffened. "Yes. Very."

Rush tipped his face toward the sky, squinting against the light. "What is he? Some sort of local wheel?"

Anna folded her arms across her chest, annoyed at his sarcastic tone. "You could say that. He's one of the richest men in the state. Certainly the richest in the Delta."

"Is that so?"

"Yes." She met his gaze evenly in challenge. "And everything he's done, he's done on his own. His daddy was a field hand who drank more often than he worked. He barely kept a roof over their heads."

"An absolute paragon," Rush muttered, taking a step toward her. "But he doesn't have everything he wants. Does he, Anna?"

"And just what's that supposed to mean?"

"Figure it out."

Her heart began to rap uncomfortably against the wall of her chest. He couldn't mean that Travis wanted...her? She thought of the look in Travis's eyes as he'd gazed at her, of the way she'd felt as he'd driven out of sight.

She shook her head. The thought was as ludicrous as it was insulting. She lifted her chin. "Travis and I are just friends. Good friends. He's never made advances. He never would."

"Just because he hasn't made one, doesn't mean he hasn't wanted to." Rush leaned toward her, so close she felt his breath stir against her cheek. "Better be careful, Annabelle. The guy was practically salivating. But maybe that's what you want."

She glared at him. "What damn business of yours is my and Travis's relationship?"

"None." Rush returned her glare, and Anna had the sense that he was furious. "Just trying to help you out. Thought maybe you'd set your sights on this guy."

"Well, I haven't. We're just friends."

One corner of his mouth lifted in a sardonic smile. "Right."

Anger and frustration bloomed inside her. She placed her fists on her hips and faced him. "You probably think men and women can't even be friends because of—"

"Sex," he finished for her. "They can't. It always raises its ugly head. One or the other of the 'friends' is always hurt."

Had she hurt Travis in some way? Was that why Travis had seemed so sad? She narrowed her eyes. *Nonsense. Rush Cousins was nothing but a trouble-maker. And for whatever reason, he wanted to aggravate her.*

Well, he wouldn't, Anna vowed. Not this time.

"You don't know anything about me and Travis. We grew up together. It was Travis who taught me to ride a two-wheel bike and to drive a standard shift. It was Travis who took me to my senior prom when no one else asked, and it was Travis who held my hand at Daddy's funeral.''

"I know what I see."

The blood rushed to her head, the urge to hit him along with it. She took a deep breath, fighting to keep her cool, knowing she'd already lost it. "This conversation is totally inappropriate. Excuse me."

She moved to brush by him. He caught her arm, stopping her, forcing her to look at him. She felt the heat of his fingers to the center of her being. "Take your hand off me."

He tightened his grip. "Totally inappropriate because I'm the hired help?"

Anna cocked up her chin, furious. With him. With herself for allowing him to get to her, for almost kissing him not thirty minutes ago. For wishing he would kiss her now. "Yes," she lied. "Because you're the hired help."

"You are one cold princess."

"And I could fire you."

"You could." He smiled, the curving of his lips slow and confident. "But you won't."

"Are you so sure?"

His gaze lowered to her mouth for one dizzying moment, then he lifted it back to hers. "Yes. You need me, Anna. You hate it, but it's true."

He slid his hand from her elbow to the curve of her neck. The blood thrummed in her head, her limbs grew heavy. "No," she whispered. "You're wrong."

"What do you need, Annabelle Ames?" he asked, his voice thick. "What do you want?"

"You're going to end up alone, Anna. Almost forty, and all dried up already."

She brought her hands to Rush's chest, curling her fingers into the sweat-dampened weave of his T-shirt, panic squeezing at her heart and lungs. "Don't you want to be held? To be cherished? Loved?"

She fought back Lowell's words, fought the way they made her feel, alone and frightened. She sucked in a deep, painful breath. "I don't need anything," she whispered, cursing the huskiness of her voice. "Especially from you."

"No?" He cupped her chin in his palm and stared deeply into her eyes. "I don't believe you. Not for a moment."

"That's your problem, isn't it?"

"Maybe it is," he murmured. "And maybe I'd better solve it." He lowered his eyes to her mouth and for one heart-stopping moment, she thought he was going to kiss her. Then he dropped his hand. "But today I've got a roof to repair. And I'm still on the clock. See you around."

Anna watched him walk away, tears burning the backs of her eyes. She despised him, she thought. She wanted him off her property. She wanted to never see him again.

She opened her mouth, his dismissal on the tip of her tongue. She swallowed it. She couldn't fire him, as much as she wanted to. She needed him. Ashland needed him.

Anna swore. But worse, much worse, was the fact that he'd been right. She wanted him. To kiss her. To hold and stroke and make love to her.

Anna pressed her lips tightly together to keep them from trembling. What a joke. He neither needed nor wanted her. And what if he did? She would only lie there, as stiff and dry as an old cypress board.

Memories of other times, of other men, filled her head. Her fiancé's sarcasm. Spencer McKee's laughter. Lee Fuller's violence. Anna shuddered, the images playing through her head like an obscene kaleidoscope.

Damn Rush Cousins for making her feel this way again. Damn him for making her remember. Before he'd come to Ashland, she'd been fine. Satisfied with her life. Resigned to her loveless future. She'd managed to tuck away the hurt, the disappointments, managed to tuck them into a quiet place where they hadn't the ability to touch her.

They touched now. Stinging, burning.

And they refused to be tucked away. They refused to let her be. Tears welled in her eyes once more, only this time she didn't have the strength to fight them off.

Chapter Four

Anna shelved her pride and let Rush work on the roof alone. She couldn't bear working beside him, feeling his every glance, continually wondering what he was thinking and cursing herself for her own ridiculous thoughts. Instead, she began repairing walls that had been damaged by water from the leaking roof.

Consequently they'd barely spoken in the week since their argument over her and Travis's relationship. She'd continued to prepare and serve him his lunch; they'd even eaten their sandwiches together a couple of times. But there'd been no arguments or companionable discussions. No almost-kisses. Rush had been as quiet, as removed, as she. Almost as if he, too, still stung over their last meeting.

Anna made a sound of self-disgust. Right. What did he have to be embarrassed or angry over? He'd had the last word. The last laugh. He hadn't made a fool of himself.

Anna muttered an oath, viciously digging at the plaster wall. But she *had* made a fool of herself. She still was. Because no matter how she tried, no matter where she was or what she was involved in, she couldn't get him off of her mind.

The nights were the worst. Hot and still. The air heavy with moisture and the scents of the Delta. Night after night she lay in bed and stared at the ceiling, her thoughts on him, unable to sleep for imagining him naked, his flesh slick from the heat, quivering with arousal.

Unable to sleep for wondering what it would be like to have his heat over her, inside her.

Pretty hot thoughts for a forty-year-old spinster with a history of frigidity.

This had to stop, Anna told herself, slamming the hammer down on the end of the chisel. She had to find a way to make it stop. Otherwise she—

"Hey."

Anna whirled around. Rush stood in the doorway, leaning against the jamb. His T-shirt was drenched with sweat and clung to his muscular chest. He'd tied a bandana across his forehead to keep sweat from dripping into his eyes, and as she gazed at him he slipped it off, tucked it into his back jeans pocket and ran his fingers through his damp hair. She followed the movement of his hands, a sweet, heavy ache building deep inside her.

She brought her gaze back to his and he smiled, slow and easy. The ache tightened, and she muttered an oath. "Hey to you."

Blue came barreling in from the kitchen. He stopped in front of Rush, his tail wagging so hard his whole backside shook. Rush squatted down and scratched the dog's ears and chest. With a whine of pleasure and submission, Blue rolled onto his back. Anna scowled. *Turncoat.* She would have to have a serious talk with the beast.

But, she wondered, who would have a serious talk with her?

Rush scratched the dog for another moment, then straightened. "Glad I'm not that wall," he said, eyeing the chisel and hammer. "Looks to me like you're trying to kill it."

She arched her eyebrows coolly. "Actually, I was imagining you were. The wall, that is."

He laughed and started for her. Like a cat, she thought. Quietly, fluidly and with the unshakable determination of a hunter stalking its prey.

She fought the urge to take the mouse's way and run. Instead, she turned back to the wall. Placing the chisel at the edge of the water damage, she struck it with the hammer. Hard. Bits of plaster tumbled to the floor.

"I guess that means you're still ticked off."

"Not at all," she answered, once more slamming the hammer onto the chisel.

Unperturbed, Rush leaned against the wall, forcing her to stop working and look at him. "It's been mighty quiet around here this week."

"Peaceful," she countered.

"You didn't miss our invigorating exchanges? Not even a little?"

"Invigorating exchanges?" she repeated incredulously. "Is that what you call them?"

"Sure." He grinned. "What would you call them?"

"Aggravating. Annoying."

"Exciting. Exhilarating."

"Maybe to you." She made a sound of frustration. "Did you need something?"

He leaned toward her, his eyes alight with mischief. "Loaded question, Annabelle."

Her pulse scrambled, and she called herself an idiot. "Then I'll be more direct. You're keeping me from my work."

He moved his gaze over her face. "How about a truce?"

"Doubtful."

"The roof's finished."

She sucked in a quick, surprised breath. "What?"

"The roof," he repeated, looking smug. "It's finished."

"But that's...impossible. I'd scheduled several more weeks...." She scowled at him. "If this is some sort of sick joke, you're in very big trouble."

Rush laughed and shrugged. "No joke, babe. It's done."

The biggest job of the summer, Anna thought, stunned. Complete. No more leaks, no more crumbling, bulging walls. No more lying awake at night worrying about the damage the next rain would bring.

And finished in half the time she'd thought it would take. At this rate, they could very possibly make every repair on the list before she went back to teaching in August.

Anna tipped her head back and laughed, feeling as if a huge weight had been lifted from her shoulders. "I can't believe it. This is...wonderful! It's...great. I don't know how to thank you."

"A little warmth," Rush teased, reaching out and lightly caressing her cheek. "An occasional smile. Something cold to drink." He dropped his hand and smiled wickedly. "I'm an uncomplicated, simple man."

Anna laughed again, her cheek still warm from his touch. "As uncomplicated as a wolf."

"I resent that."

He looked entirely too pleased with himself, Anna thought, setting aside the chisel and hammer. Smug. Cocky. But the way she felt right now, she wouldn't care if he thought he was God's gift to women in general and her in particular.

She smiled. "I'll never doubt you again."

Rush leaned toward her. "Watch what you say, Annabelle Ames. Your promises may come back to haunt you."

She laughed and shook her head. "I still can't believe you just showed up here at Ashland. Out of nowhere. I'd already resigned myself to another high-school student."

"Not out of nowhere," he murmured. "Boston. Remember?"

She laughed again and fluttered her lashes. "As far as a good Southern belle like myself is concerned, that is nowhere. Didn't you know, civilization ends at the Mason-Dixon Line?"

"Why, Annabelle, I do believe you're giddy."

"I'm not the giddy type. Ask anyone." Even as the words passed her lips, she had to admit she did feel...giddy. And light-headed, and about as steady as a sixteen-year-old.

She laughed again, not caring that he probably thought her one of those neurotic Southern women Tennessee Williams had written about. "I have fresh-squeezed lemonade in the icebox. And some tea cookies. I'll meet you outside in five.''

Instead of waiting for Anna on the gallery, Rush chose a lush, shady spot under the magnolia that stood closest to the house. Slivers of sunlight peeked through the thick canopy of leaves, dappling the ground with pinpoints of light.

Rush picked up a magnolia petal, shed from one of the blossoms above. He rubbed the large petal between his fingers, enjoying its soft, waxy surface. He held it to his nose. Its fragrance was delicate, sweet yet citrusy, too; its color a pure, virginal white.

Rush drew his eyebrows together, holding the flower to his nose once more. Although magnolia blossoms looked sturdy, they were really quite fragile. They bruised when handled, withering at even the most gentle caress.

The magnolia was not quite as it appeared, he thought, smiling to himself. Just as Annabelle was not completely the woman she appeared to be. She continued to surprise and mystify him. She continued to intrigue him.

Rush laughed out loud, thinking of her offer of lemonade and tea cookies. What the hell was a tea cookie, anyway? Certainly not something he would associate with a woman wearing work boots and wielding a chisel and hammer.

Yet in many ways Annabelle was old-fashioned, ladylike and genteel. He thought of the music box, of the porcelain belle inside. He could envision Anna that way, dressed in a picture hat and hoop skirt, her arms full of flowers.

Just as he could picture her atop a roof in the dead of summer, nailing the hell out of roofing tiles.

And her thumb, he thought, smiling at the memory and at her as she emerged from Ashland carrying a tray. He tossed the magnolia aside, and watched Anna as she crossed the lawn to meet him. He liked the way she moved, slowly and fluidly, with an athletic sort of grace. She didn't swing her hips or sashay; her stride was long and full of purpose.

Anna stopped before him, her face flushed. She'd freed her hair from its clip and brushed it until it glowed golden in the waning sunlight. He smiled up at her. "This tree's been taunting me for over a week now. I promised when I finished the roof I would reward myself by sitting in its shade."

She hesitated, glancing quickly back at the gallery.

"Come on." He patted the grass beside him. "I promise I won't bite."

The color in her cheeks deepened. "I wasn't worried about that."

"I must be doing something wrong."

She laughed lightly and set the tray on the ground, then took a seat herself. "I hope it's not too tart for you," she said, pouring him a glass of the beverage and handing it to him.

He took the glass; their fingers brushed. He found her gaze and held it. "Not to worry, Annabelle. I like mine tart."

She flushed again and dragged her gaze away. He watched as she nervously sipped her lemonade, then fiddled with the hem of her shorts.

What would it take to draw her out? he wondered, studying her. What would it feel like to have her trust? The way Travis Gentry did.

He needed her trust. He needed her to open up if he was ever going to determine if he had a place here at Ashland. But at this moment he didn't give a damn about unearthing his past. At this moment, all he was interested in was Anna, the woman.

"This is my favorite time of year, even with the heat," she murmured, not looking at him. "Because of the magnolias."

"You don't say."

Her lips tipped up at the corners. "Did you know that it's the heat that makes their scent so sweet and so potent? Without it they'd bloom but be almost odorless."

"They do smell heavenly."

She tilted her head back, gazing at the thick foliage above. Her neck arched with the movement and her hair fell away from her face, revealing the slender column of her throat. Her skin was as smooth and white as the blossoms above, and the urge to touch her raced over him. He told himself to get a grip.

"You've chosen a poor spot for our celebration," she said. "This tree has a rather dangerous history." She shifted her gaze to his, a small smile pulling at the corners of her mouth. "It's called Sweethearts' Magnolia."

He grinned and plucked a long blade of grass from the ground beside him and twirled it between his fingers. "That does sound dangerous."

She turned her gaze once more to the canopy of green above. "Three generations of Ames brides were proposed to under these branches, and it's rumored several others were simply seduced here."

"You'll give me ideas."

"I doubt that."

"Sweethearts' Magnolia," he repeated.

"And we're not even friends. You see the irony."

He flashed her a quick smile. "We could remedy that."

She arched her eyebrows. "I thought you didn't believe men and women could be friends?"

Because of sex. Rush curved his fingers around the blade of grass, arousal tightening in his gut. "Maybe I've changed my mind."

She picked up her glass, but didn't sip. "But that's a woman's prerogative."

"And here I thought you believed in equality between the sexes."

"You have me there, Rush Cousins." She shifted her gaze back to Ashland, her cheeks rosy with color.

Rush followed her gaze, attempting to see what she did when she looked at the house, attempting to feel what she felt. Her face changed in subtle ways, softening. The expression in her eyes had the glow of pride and passion, of belonging.

He'd never felt that way about anyone or anything. He hadn't wanted to for so long, he couldn't even remember how it felt to yearn to belong.

But still, looking at Anna now, he thought he could understand. "This place is in your blood, isn't it?"

She met his eyes. "You could say that." She drained the remainder of her glass of lemonade, then set it aside. "People around here think I'm crazy for loving Ashland so much, for being so determined to hold on to her. You probably do, too."

"I don't think that at all."

She smiled. "Thanks."

"You're welcome."

She looked away again and silence enveloped them for a moment. It was a comfortable quiet, the kind they had never before experienced together. And Anna began to relax. Really relax. Rush saw her guard begin to slip: the line of her shoulders softened, as did the curve of her jaw. She lost the nervous edginess, the sharp defensiveness. Even her mouth seemed softer. Pouty, kissable.

"Tell me what it feels like," he murmured, trailing his fingers across the mat of grass.

"What what feels like?" she asked, drawing her eyebrows together in question.

"Belonging."

She paused, the blue of her eyes becoming softer still. But this time with sympathy. With the understanding of someone who had experienced her share of alienation.

"But surely," she continued, "you have somewhere you belong...people you go back to."

Rush thought of the years spent alone, thought of the struggle to find a place he fit. To find a place where he was comfortable with himself and his history.

"I do. But it's not the same as the connection you have with Ashland. With the South, even. If it were, I wouldn't be here."

She nodded. "You have a way of putting things that makes sense to me."

Rush propped himself up on an elbow. "A compliment from the mistress of Ashland," he teased. "Could it be?"

She tipped her head back and laughed, and the sweet, throaty sound played over his senses. "Am I that bad?"

He grinned. "Much worse, actually."

She laughed again, then shook her head, her expression growing serious. "I don't know how to explain my feelings. I feel at home here. And safe. I feel this... sense of urgency when I think of Ashland. And when I'm here, I feel peace."

"Have you ever lived anywhere else?"

"In Memphis for a couple years. I got a teaching position at a prestigious girls' school. It was too good to turn down, and I thought moving away was what I was supposed to do."

"But you came home."

"Ashland drew me back." She tipped her face to the sky and drew in a lungful of the sweet summer air. "I don't think anywhere in the world could smell as sweet as Ashland in June."

As if realizing how much she'd revealed of herself, she blushed and lowered her eyes. Rush moved his gaze over her profile. He liked her this way—soft and flushed and smiling. How, only days ago, had he thought her plain? How had he failed to notice her high cheekbones and straight, delicately chiseled nose; her soft, smooth skin and surprisingly full mouth?

A mouth meant for kissing.

Awareness barreled through him, catching him off guard, stunning him. He sucked in a quick breath and dragged his gaze from her too-kissable mouth.

"Tell me more about your life here at Ashland. Your parents. Your childhood."

Anna drew her knees to her chest and rested her chin on them. She turned her face to his. "When I think of my childhood, most often I think of Daddy. He was a dreamer. A storyteller. I grew up on tales of the Old South, tales of ladies and gentlemen and codes of honor. I was weaned on heroic tales of the Ames ancestors."

She laughed lightly. "Daddy took his position as Joshua Ames, master of Ashland, very seriously. Serious in the sense that he believed the stories himself. He believed in his own...stature."

She turned her gaze back to the house, with its huge square columns and massive entablature. "Unfortunately, he didn't have the drive to back up his dreams. By the time I stepped in after Mama died, there was almost nothing left. Daddy had sold off everything to maintain the Ames image and life-style. If not for Mama's hard work and business acumen, Ashland would have come to the state it is in today years sooner."

Anna drew her eyebrows together. "I never saw his weakness. I never knew that it was Mama who ran things, Mama who held us all together."

"You didn't want to."

"I guess not. I guess I believed the image, too." She lifted her shoulders. "Daddy gave me my love of this place, my love of the South. Mama gave me my strength."

"But it was different for Lowell." Rush regretted the words the moment he uttered them. He saw her stiffen, felt her withdrawal as an almost physical thing.

"Tell me one of your father's stories," he said quickly, cursing having mentioned her brother, hoping he hadn't ruined the mood.

"You'd really like to hear one?" When he nodded, she smiled. "Okay, I'll tell you my favorite." She sat up and drew her knees to her chest. "The story's about an extremely wealthy and flamboyant planter from Louisiana. On the occasion of the simultaneous wedding of two of his daughters, he imported large spi-

ders from China and had them set free in the oak alley
that led to the house. The spiders spun great webs, and
the morning of the weddings, servants were given bel-
lows of gold and silver dust. They coated the webs, and
that night the couples were led by torchlight under the
glittering canopy."

"Very romantic."

Annabelle sighed. It wasn't the sigh of a young girl's
longing, but of a grown woman surrounded by bittersweet memories. The sound tugged at him in a way that
was both unfamiliar and warm.

"Daddy told me that story for the first time when I
was four. He promised he would do that for me when
I married. The whole thing." A flicker of regret crossed
her features. "As a little girl I had no idea of the cost
of something like that, or of the fact that I might . . .
never marry."

Why hadn't she? Rush wondered, cocking his head.
She was attractive and smart; she was from a prestigious family. How had a girl with so many traditional
ideas grown into such a nontraditional woman?

He thought of her friend Travis Gentry, and drew his
eyebrows together. He recalled the warmth in her eyes
as she'd gazed at the other man, recalled the way they'd
embraced. Maybe the right man had never asked. Rush
frowned, irritated by his own thoughts.

Annabelle tipped her head and met his eyes. "Daddy
told me a lot of fantastic stories. Ones about duels being fought for honor, about great balls and star-crossed
lovers."

"Why, Annabelle," Rush drawled, "you're a romantic."

She lifted her eyebrows in genuine surprise. "Not at
all."

"You are." He leaned toward her. "And a dreamer. Just like your father."

"I'm not."

Rush reached up and curled his fingers into her hair. It felt like dandelion down against his skin. "Then what are you, Ms. Annabelle Ames?"

She drew in a shuddering breath, fighting for equilibrium. For control. "Why, I'm . . . practical. Logical. Pragma—"

"Uh-uh." He tightened his fingers in her golden hair. "You're a romantic." He curved his hand around the back of her neck, inching her face toward his. "Soft . . . womanly."

Anna battled for an even breath. Dear God, she felt womanly. And soft. And sexual.

Impossible. She was none of those things. She shook her head. "I assure you, I—"

"Oh no, Annabelle. I have your number now." He drew her face closer. "Remember what you said the other day about Yankees?"

She bit back a whimper, even as she found herself leaning toward him. "That we would have won the war, but you Yankees cheated?"

Rush laughed softly and moved his fingers in slow, mesmerizing circles. "No, Annabelle. You called us brash. And we are. Brash. And bold." He lowered his voice. "We take what we want."

Anna pressed her hands against his chest, her heart thundering. She searched for something to say, something bright or clever, something that would bring her crashing back to reality Her mind was blank save for the need for his mouth, his touch.

"Do you know what I want?"

She hoped she did, but she shook her head, the breath shuddering past her lips.

"This."

Rush brought his mouth to hers. Softly. Carefully. As if testing her response, testing his own. He brushed his lips across hers; with the tip of his tongue he tasted the tip of hers.

She couldn't judge his response, but hers was cataclysmic. The blood rushed to her head, the breath from her lungs. Parts of her body that had never known heat burst into flame. She ached; she yearned.

She wanted more.

Her head fell back and a moan escaped from deep in her throat. She clutched at his T-shirt, alternately pulling him closer and pushing him away.

He lifted his head, and she made a sound of protest. She opened her eyes to find his gaze on her, his expression hooded.

He hadn't enjoyed kissing her, she thought, self-doubt worming its way into her consciousness, replacing the delight of a moment ago. He regretted it. He knew the truth about her.

It hurt. It hurt so badly she thought she might die. She curled her fingers in the soft weave of his shirt. "I thought you wanted to be friends," she whispered, trying to sound glib and failing miserably.

"But I don't believe men and women can be friends." Rush smiled wickedly and tumbled her to her back. "Because of sex."

He lowered his mouth to hers once more, only this time he didn't test; he didn't request. He plundered. He took. And she followed, without thought or fear, self-doubt expunged by arousal.

Wild sensations, foreign and exhilarating, raced through her. The blood pounded in her head until all disappeared but its wild, primitive beat. What was happening to her? she wondered dizzily. She'd never wanted like this . . . had never behaved so . . . wantonly.

Anna sucked in a deep breath. The smell of the grass and the earth, of the flowers and the sun, filled her head. And with them the smell of man. This man. Of Rush. He smelled strong. Musky, like a man who had worked all day in the sun. Like a man should.

She drew in another breath, growing drunk on the scent. Drunk and unbearably wet.

Gasping, she tugged him closer, frantically digging her fingers into his shoulders, opening her mouth more, wanting him closer, deeper.

"Anna . . . Anna . . ." Rush curled his fingers in her hair, spread out on the ground around her head. The softness of her breasts flattened against his chest as he pressed himself against her. He answered her plea, deepening the kiss, his tongue stroking and twining with hers.

Yet deeper wasn't enough. Rush moved his hands from her hair to her face. He splayed his fingers over her cheeks, stunned at his response to her. At her response to him. He never would have suspected that beneath Anna's quiet, guarded reserve teemed a volcano of passion.

He never would have suspected she could ignite such an answering passion in him.

He was neither young nor inexperienced. Since he'd been old enough to care, women had been drawn to him. And he to them. Sex had come early—and naturally. But this . . . this didn't feel real. It felt super-real.

He wanted this woman. Beyond reason or good sense. In a way he hadn't wanted since those first desperate encounters in his youth. Or maybe ever.

Why? He tore his mouth from hers. What made her so special? What made holding her feel so new? So extraordinary?

Instinct warned him to go slow; he ignored instinct and found her breasts, cupping them, moving his thumbs across her erect nipples.

Anna froze, a memory from her fifteenth summer barreling into her head, and with it the urge to run. Arousal evaporated, was replaced by fear, icy cold and numbing.

The boy's weight pressed her back against the naked field. A stone bit viciously into her shoulder blade, and she cried out. But not in pain. In terror. She pushed frantically, ineffectually, against the boy's chest, her breath coming in shallow gasps.

He pawed at her, his hands clutching at her breasts, hurting her. From somewhere outside herself she heard the scream of a truck barreling past, the cry of a mockingbird, the rasp of a zipper being yanked down.

She heard Macy calling her to lunch.

Anna squeezed her eyes shut, trying to force the memory from her head. Trying to rid herself of the panic coursing through her. She wasn't fifteen years old, she told herself. She was in control. She knew exactly what to do—where to strike and how—should she be attacked.

This was Rush touching her, not Lee Fuller. She wasn't being attacked. She'd invited Rush's touch, his kiss. She'd enjoyed it almost desperately.

For a moment. Only a moment.

Tears of frustration and disappointment welled in her eyes, and she wedged her hands between them. Dear Lord, how had she allowed herself to get into this situation? What had she been thinking? She couldn't do this. She didn't want it. She'd been crazy to think this time would be different.

A sob rising in her throat, she pushed against Rush's chest.

"Anna?" He lifted his head, his expression dazed, his breathing labored. For a long moment, he gazed down at her, confused. "What's wrong? What's—"

"Let me go." She squirmed beneath him, fighting the panic, fighting the fear pressing in on her. Fear that he wouldn't let her go. That she would have to fight him. That, in the end, she wouldn't be strong enough to free herself.

What would she do if that happened? she wondered, hysteria rising like a bile inside her. This time, how would she live through it?

"Anna?" Rush curved his fingers around her shoulders. "Did I do something to...tell me what I—"

"Get off me, I said!" The panic clawed at her, and she flailed her fists against his chest. "Now, dammit!"

Rush rolled off her, his expression stunned. Without giving him a chance to speak, Anna jumped up and raced for the safety of Ashland.

Chapter Five

Hours later, Anna paced. The brilliant light of midday had been replaced by the purple of late afternoon. The time since she'd run from Rush had passed with excruciating slowness. She'd paced and raged and cried; she'd cursed a past that refused to let her out of its grip.

She paused beside one of the parlor windows that faced the front of the house and gazed out at Sweethearts' Magnolia, at the spot that she and Rush had occupied such a short time ago. Tears choked her. How had she allowed herself to get into that situation? She knew better. Anna covered her face with her hands. And how had she believed that it would be different with this man? With Rush?

But it had been different—it had been *worse*. Anna made a sound of humiliation and pain, shame washing over her. Because she'd felt so deeply. Because she'd wanted him so much.

Had she really arched and moaned and clawed at him? He'd done nothing more than brush his mouth against hers, and she'd all but charged him.

She'd never wanted anyone the way she'd wanted Rush. No wonder she'd hoped . . . hoped that maybe, just maybe this time, she would be able to be with a man without either freezing or panicking.

Anna moved closer to the window. She saw that Rush had brought the tray up to the gallery and left it there for her. She laid her fingers on the window, remembering what Rush had felt like under her fingers, wishing she touched him now instead of the unresponsive glass.

The tears spilled over and slipped slowly down her cheeks. She turned away from the window. Would she ever be free of the past? Would she ever be able to forget and go on?

For one brief, exciting moment, she had forgotten. For that one moment she had known what it was to be a whole woman.

A knock sounded on the door, and Anna swung toward the foyer, her heart in her throat. Rush. He'd come to talk to her about what had happened between them.

She clasped her hands together. She didn't want to see him. Not now. Not yet. She sucked in a deep breath. Maybe never.

He knocked again. She owed him an explanation. After all, one moment she'd been moaning in his arms; the next, flailing against his chest with her fists.

Her cheeks burned. How would she face him? What would she say when she did?

Anna glanced toward the back of the house. She could hide. Slip into her bedroom, close and lock the door. As the urge to do just that surged through her, she fisted her fingers. If she did, she would have sunk to a new and embarrassing low—hiding like a child. She shook her head. She couldn't do that and still retain a shred of her dignity.

Besides, he knew she was here.

Wiping the moisture from her cheeks, she lifted her chin and crossed to the door. She had to face Rush, just as she had to face life. She had to be strong. In control. She wished she'd had time to prepare an explanation, time to prepare herself to face him. She hadn't. She would simply tell him that what had happened between them had been a mistake. One she expected never to happen again.

Grasping the knob, Anna swung the huge old door open. "Rush, I—"

The woman on the other side of the door lifted her coal-black eyebrows in amusement. "Honey, I ain't no Rush, but I am interested in who he is. You look like you seen union troops comin' up the road."

"Macy! I didn't expect ... You're not—" Anna bit back the words and flung her arms around the other woman, squeezing her tightly.

Macy Taylor was the wife of the plantation's last overseer and had been housekeeper at Ashland the whole time Anna had been growing up. Eighty-some years old and big as a mule, Anna loved her like a second mother.

And at this moment there was no one Anna would have liked to see more. Tears of relief pricked at her eyes, and she fought them back. "It's so good to see you," Anna murmured.

Macy drew away from her and searched her expression with eyes that saw too much. Anna felt herself flush and cursed the telling color.

"You gonna let your old Macy in? I'm too old and too fat to be standin' out in this heat."

Shaking her head, Anna drew the other woman in. "Of course. And you're not too old for anything."

Macy laughed, the throaty sound full of love of life. "Are you saying I'm fat, child?" The big woman clucked her tongue. "Never did have enough respect for your elders. Neither you or that sassy brother of yours."

"I said no such thing, as you very well know." Anna smiled and led Macy to the front parlor. She helped the older woman onto an ancient, battered settee. "By any chance is that corn bread I smell?" Anna motioned to the basket Macy clutched on her lap.

"Corn-bread muffins and honey butter." Macy thrust the basket at Anna. "I thought we could have some tea and a chat. I like mine sweet. Don't you forget."

As if she could. Anna shook her head in amusement and started for the kitchen.

A few minutes later Anna sat across from Macy. "I thought your doctor told you to cut down on your sugar intake?"

"He did." Macy selected a muffin and slathered it with the honey butter. "My fats, too."

"And?" Anna eyed the muffin and tea meaningfully.

Macy snorted. "The good Lord's seen fit for me to live this long, no uppity boy gonna tell me how to live now. No sir."

The "uppity boy" was in his thirties and had been the sole physician in Ames since his own father had retired over ten years ago. Anna smiled. "Then by all means, have another muffin."

"Sassy," the women muttered, looking Anna squarely in the eye. "Now tell your old Macy what's troublin' you."

Macy had always been able to see when something bothered her. Always. And now, Anna knew, she would be able to see through anything less than the truth. Even if she didn't comment on Anna's evasion, she would know. It hurt Anna to have Macy think she didn't trust her or care enough to share her feelings with her.

But this she couldn't share.

Anna tried to smile and failed. "Nothing's wrong. I'm just tired. We've...I've been working too hard. That's all. So," she continued quickly, hoping Macy would let a change of subject slip past, "are you planning to spend July in Memphis again this year? I know your sister must enjoy having you for such a nice long visit."

Macy narrowed her eyes and cleared her throat. Anna sighed. Macy didn't buy her story. She hadn't been distracted by the introduction of her trip to her sister's. Sometimes Macy pushed, sometimes she didn't. It was one of the ways the feisty housekeeper had kept both her and Lowell in line as children. Anna held her breath, wondering which she would do this time, praying she would let the subject drop.

The older woman made a sound of disgust. "I've been tellin' you that for years. You're too thin. You work too hard. But do you listen to Macy? No, sir." She polished off her muffin and reached for another.

"You need to find yourself a good man, Annabelle Ames. Settle down and have some babies. Women ain't supposed to live this way." She wagged a finger at her. "Listen to your Macy before it's too late."

Before it's too late.

The words resounded in Anna's head. Usually she pooh-poohed Macy's old-fashioned sentiments, her concerns. Usually she looked around her and felt complete. Felt like what she was doing was worthwhile, like it was enough.

But today, her love of Ashland wasn't enough. Today, she felt lonely and alone. Today she wondered if it wasn't already too late.

Not wanting Macy to see the glaze of tears in her eyes, she shifted her gaze, pretending interest in a muffin.

"Seen that no-account brother of yours?"

Anna nodded but still didn't meet the other woman's eyes. Lowell had been Macy's baby, too. She knew how much it hurt the other woman to see him so bitter and unhappy.

"Damn shame." Macy shook her head slowly. "Came by to see me, too. Didn't look good. No, sir. Fed him a meal and read him some Scripture. But he didn't seem to find no peace in it."

Anna reached across the coffee table and covered Macy's big hand with her own. "I'm sorry."

"You say that like you had somethin' to do with the way your brother turned out. You didn't." Macy squeezed her fingers, then released them and rested her full weight against the settee's back. It groaned in response. "Some days I'd like to take that daddy of yours an'…" She shook her head and folded her hands in her lap. "But that ain't the Lord's way."

Anna opened her mouth, and Macy waved her words aside. "There's nothin' more that needs to be said on that subject, child. Tell me instead about this stranger you hired."

For the first time in several minutes, Anna thought of Rush and their encounter earlier. Her cheeks heated, and she clasped her hands together. "There's not much to tell. His name's Rush Cousins and he's an experienced builder. We've already finished the roof."

"Hear tell he's from up north."

"Boston."

Macy narrowed her eyes. "Unusual name, Rush. Only known one other. Years ago."

"Was he a Yankee, too?" Anna asked innocently.

"Sassy-mouthed young'un. I thought I done raised you up better than that." Once again, she wagged a finger at Anna. "Just be careful, child."

Anna smiled. "Everybody's so worried about me these days. Do I look that fragile?"

Macy gazed at her, her dark eyes soft with concern. And affection. "I love you, Annabelle Marie Ames. You and Lowell, you're like my own babies. Don't want nothin' or nobody hurtin' my babies."

Tears sprang to Anna's eyes again, only this time she didn't try to hide them. She crossed to Macy and hugged her. "I love you, too, Macy."

Macy patted her cheek. "I best be goin'. Brady'll be callin' for me any minute. You know how he gets when I make him wait."

"That I do." Anna helped the older women up, alarmed at how their visit had fatigued her. Each time Anna saw her, Macy seemed to have aged a little more. And they saw each other every couple of weeks, sometimes more often than that. Anna couldn't imagine a day when Macy wouldn't be a phone call away.

"Big storm expected tonight," Macy said as Anna opened the front door. "Sky's already changin'."

Anna looked up at the sky, at the gathering clouds, then back at Macy. "Don't worry about me, I've already battened down the hatches." They stepped out onto the gallery. "I've got plenty of bottled water and candles and..."

Rush stood on a ladder not ten feet from them, examining damage to the gallery ceiling. Anna gazed at him, her mouth dry, her palms damp. Dear Lord, not now. She wasn't ready for this, she wasn't—

Rush turned and met her eyes. Anna's heart stopped, then started again with a vengeance. He didn't smile or speak; his expression gave away nothing of his thoughts or feelings.

Anna sucked in a quick breath and tore her gaze from Rush's. She turned back to Macy, fighting for an air of normalcy. "Macy, this is...Rush Cousins. Rush, this is Macy Taylor. An old friend."

Macy moved her gaze speculatively over him. "So you're the Yankee. From Boston."

"Yes, ma'am," he said, flashing Macy a brilliant smile. "Pleased to meet you, too."

Just then, Brady drove up and honked. Macy didn't move. She continued to stare at Rush, and Anna said a silent thank-you when Brady honked again, this time with little patience. She'd seen the speculation in Macy's eyes, and she didn't want to give her too much opportunity to figure out what was going on.

A kiss, Anna thought, disgusted with herself. They'd shared a kiss; nothing else was going on.

Macy held tightly to Anna's arm as they descended the steps and crossed to the drive. "There's somethin' mighty familiar about that boy."

Anna shook her head. "I don't know what it could be. He just arrived in Ames three weeks ago."

"Powerful handsome."

Anna flushed. "I hadn't noticed."

Macy chuckled and let Anna help her into the battered old sedan. Once settled, the older woman looked at Anna in knowing amusement. "Child, if that man doesn't set your panties on fire, you ain't alive."

"Macy!"

The older woman chuckled again. "I've lived too long and seen too much to pitty-pat around the truth. You need a man, an' there's a good one right under your nose."

Beside Macy, Brady sighed, rested his head against the seat back and closed his eyes. Anna bit back a smile. Like she did, Brady knew from experience that when Macy had a point to make, there was no rushing her.

"First of all, Macy, I don't 'need' a man, and secondly, how did we go from 'be careful' to 'snag him quick' with nothing more than an introduction? You don't know anything about him."

"But I do." She folded her big hands primly in her lap. "You can tell a lot about a man from his eyes. And smile. I can tell that this is a good one."

Anna made a sound of exasperation. "Macy—"

"Mark my words, child, and don't let him get away."

"You drive me crazy, you know that?" Anna bent and pressed a kiss to Macy's soft, dark cheek. "But I love you anyway."

Macy's eyes filled. "I love you, too, sugar sweet."

After exchanging a few pleasantries with Brady, Anna watched the two drive off. When the car disappeared from sight, she turned to Ashland.

And Rush.

Face him now, she told herself. Now, while feeling buoyed by Macy's visit. Confront the situation head-on.

Calling herself a coward, Anna turned and went around to the back door.

Rush stood just beyond Ashland's circle of light. He gazed up at the house, at the bright but empty windows, and thought of Anna. Passionate and pliant in his arms, her cheeks hot with arousal, her lips, soft and parted, moist from his kisses.

She was different from any woman he'd ever known. She was smart and strong, not afraid of doing any job she had to, even one usually reserved for men. Yet at the same time she was soft, insecure, and as she'd been this afternoon, heartbreakingly vulnerable.

The women he'd known in the past had been as brash, as confident in their sexuality, as he. They'd taken the initiative in matters of the heart, going after whatever—or whomever—they wanted.

Anna was neither brash nor confident when it came to her sexuality. She kept herself, her emotions, in check; she guarded her thoughts and feelings as carefully as a mother guarded her newborn.

But this afternoon she'd been honest about what she felt in his arms. She hadn't tried to hide or pretend; she'd allowed her guard to slip away and reveal the woman she really was.

Until she'd run.

Lightning streaked across the sky above him; thunder rumbled behind it. Rush tipped his face toward the dark sky. The storm grew closer yet remained just out of reach, its passion held uneasily in check. The charged air was unnaturally still with waiting, the night unbearably hot.

Rush slipped his hands into the front pockets of his jeans and returned his gaze to Ashland. Unrelieved desire still clung to him, as heavy and hot as the night air. He wanted her still, with a ferocity that had him wondering just what the hell was happening to him.

He wasn't a stranger to women or sex. He'd learned long ago that he was a passionate man, one who enjoyed women and one whom women enjoyed.

Still, what he'd felt with Anna had been different from anything he'd ever known. It had been unexpected and cataclysmic; it had left him stunned.

And behaving like an untried boy.

Rush swore. He'd frightened her. He'd gone too fast, had ignored instinct and acted on passion. And she'd bolted. Rush flexed his fingers, the memory of the frantic way she'd pushed at his chest, of the terror in her eyes, eating at him.

It had been as if she'd feared "No" wouldn't have been enough to stop him, as if she'd feared he would have taken her against her will.

He swore again. Had he been that aggressive, that out of control? Or was it just that she didn't trust him?

Why should she? He'd lied to her. He'd come to Ashland under false pretenses, on a mission that had nothing to do with her.

And one he would complete, no matter the consequences.

Even as a thread of guilt curled through him, he thought of his trips into town at night and on his days off, thought of the questions he'd asked about the Ames family, their history, their friends.

Rush frowned. He'd found out almost nothing, and the few things that had looked like they might be leads had fizzled quickly. He was no closer to discovering the connection between himself and the music box than he'd been at the start.

And at this moment, he didn't give a damn about that. He wanted Annabelle in his arms.

She moved across one of the front windows, a slim dark silhouette against the rectangle of light, and arousal kicked him in the gut. He remembered how her breasts had felt in his palms, remembered the sound she'd made as she arched against him, remembered the way she'd parted her lips and offered him her mouth.

He should leave this alone. He should leave her alone.

A breeze stirred, deliciously cool against his damp skin. It lifted his hair and rustled the leaves above. Lightning flashed and thunder rumbled. The storm wouldn't be denied.

Rush closed the distance between him and Ashland's front door. When he reached it, he pounded on the door and called her name, pounding again when she didn't immediately answer. He tried the knob; the door swung effortlessly open.

She stood just inside the foyer. She wore a sleeveless cotton blouse. Unbuttoned at the neck, it revealed the graceful column of her neck, the swell of one breast. She'd pinned her hair up with a large clip. Her skin, smooth and milky white, gleamed with a fine sheen of sweat. Tendrils of hair had escaped the clip and clung to her damp skin.

Her eyes on his were dark with longing, her lips soft and slightly parted. Her chest rose and fell with her agitated breathing.

She wanted him. Just as badly as he wanted her. But she was afraid. He saw her fear as clearly as her arousal, and he sucked in a deep, steadying breath.

If he didn't go slowly, she would bolt again. She might, anyway.

He took a step toward her. "We need to talk."

She shook her head. "I don't want to talk. Please leave."

"What happened this afternoon, Anna? What did I do that caused you to run?"

She curved her arms around herself. "Go away."

"I can't."

"Or won't?"

"Same thing." He took another step. "What caused you to run like that? Were you afraid I would...force myself on you?"

"No...yes..." Anna shuddered. "It was a mistake. I didn't want—"

He caught her gaze, refusing to let it go. "But you did want, Annabelle. We both know it."

She shook her head. "No, I..."

A shocking flash of light rent the sky, followed by a crack of thunder. Blackness engulfed them.

Rush struggled to get his bearings. He heard Anna's quick intake of breath, heard Blue whine and scratch against a door somewhere upstairs.

Without his sense of sight, his others were heightened. He smelled the sweet flower of Anna's perfume and the scent of her sweat. And he felt her presence—

her heat, her energy, the quiet intensity that was Annabelle Ames.

He'd never experienced a sensation such as that before, and he swore softly as his eyes began to adjust.

"Blue's trapped in my bedroom," she murmured. "He's afraid of the thunder. I have to get him."

"You have candles?"

"Yes."

"I'll help you."

"I don't think—"

He reached out and caught her hand. "I'm not going to hurt you, Anna."

She met his eyes. "How do I know that?"

"I guess you're going to have to trust me."

"That's a big leap of faith you're asking for."

Especially from someone who's been burned so badly in the past. Rush saw that truth in her eyes. Anger at whoever had hurt her charged through him, and he took another step closer to her. "I've given you my word, Annabelle. I won't hurt you."

Anna hesitated. Blue whined and scratched again, this time frantically. Outside, the storm intensified. Somewhere in the house a shutter came loose and began to slam against its window frame.

Trust him? How could she trust him when just looking at him made her long to throw her doors wide and step fully into the storm? Anna caught her bottom lip between her teeth. Rush was a stranger. He made her uncomfortable and on edge. He brought forth memories she'd rather stayed locked away.

And he made her feel, made her ache. He made her want to do things she'd been too uncertain to do before.

And he made her afraid. Of failing again. Of proving to herself once and for all that she was less than a woman. Of feeling the way she had this afternoon in his arms.

And of never feeling that way again.

"Anna?"

"The candles are in the kitchen," she muttered, her heart beating out of control. "I'll show you."

She started for the kitchen; he followed. There, she took a dozen candles and holders from the pantry. He helped her light them, and she took great care that their fingers didn't touch, even jerking away and burning her hand once.

"I'll get Blue," she said, selecting a candle. "See if you can find the loose shutter."

She reached her bedroom in moments. As she opened the door, Blue lunged at her, almost toppling both her and the candle. She squatted beside him and petted him. His whole body quivered with fear.

"Poor baby," she murmured. "Whatever happened to make a big, brave dog like you so afraid of something so little bitty? You can't live in Mississippi and be afraid of rain, Baby Blue." She rubbed his chest and he whined, this time with pleasure. "It's just not natural."

"Anna?" At the sound of Rush's voice, Blue picked up his ears. "All's secure down here. Do you need me to come up?"

She glanced involuntarily at her bed, ghostly white in the darkness. She could imagine them on it, naked, writhing. Her hand began to shake, so badly she feared she would drop the candle.

She squeezed her eyes shut. What was happening to her?

"No," she managed, her voice high and breathless sounding. "I'm...coming down."

Blue beat her downstairs and by the time she stepped off the last step, the dog was wrapped around Rush's legs like a long-lost lover.

Rush stood to the right of the staircase, candle aloft to inspect a drawing hanging on the wall. Anna took a deep breath, grateful for the distraction.

"Mama did it," she said, crossing to stand beside him.

"It's you?"

"Yes, at eight."

He met her eyes, the expression in his strange. Or maybe it was the candlelight playing tricks. "Is that a music box you're holding?"

Anna shifted her gaze to the drawing and nodded. "Yes."

"It's beautiful. Very unusual."

Anna looked away, her gut twisting. "It was. Lowell sold it. He came into the house, took it and sold it."

"I'm sorry," Rush murmured. "So sorry."

"Me, too." She touched the drawing's glass lightly. "I loved that music box. It was mine. Mama had given it to me. I would never had sold it, no matter how badly I needed money. And I don't even know what Lowell used the money for."

"Who knows? Maybe it will come back to you." Rush touched her cheek lightly; she felt the caress like a brand.

Anna turned away from the drawing and crossed to the small side table by the stairs. She set the candle on it, unable to hold it steady another moment. She faced Rush once more. "It would take a miracle."

"A small one."

"Even a small one would cost more than I have."
She cleared her throat. "Thank you for taking care of
that shutter for me. I appreciate it."

"But I can go now?"

She clasped her hands in front of her. "Yes."

"Sorry, babe." He crossed the foyer in three long
strides, placing his candle next to hers. "I'm not leaving until we talk about this afternoon. And you're going to be honest with me."

She cocked up her chin. "Pretty damn presumptuous of you."

"Then try this. I want you. You want me. We had
something great going this afternoon. What happened
to end it?"

She sucked in a quick breath, hoping to offset the
wild beating of her heart. "Are you this direct with all
women?"

"Yes." He closed the remaining inches between
them, stopping so close she had tip her face up to meet
his gaze. "What's the matter, m'lady? Too bold? Not
gentlemanly enough for you?"

Anna narrowed her eyes. He was an arrogant boor.
A pushy, overconfident...Yankee. For a moment she'd
considered telling him the truth. Had considered
opening herself to him. She wouldn't open herself to
him now if it meant saving her own life.

She lifted her chin another notch. "What happened
this afternoon was a mistake. A...moment of weakness. For both of us. I expect it not to happen again."

Rush's jaw tightened. Anger darkened his eyes, and
she knew she'd pushed the wrong buttons.

"You *expect* it not to happen again? Like you're
giving me an order?" He lowered his voice. "I may
work for you, Annabelle. But I'm not a servant."

She drew in a quick breath. "I didn't mean to imply that you were. I meant, I don't *want* it to happen again."

Rush laughed. "Liar."

Heat burned her cheeks. "Get out of my house."

Instead of doing as she asked, he leaned a fraction closer to her. "You never answered my original question. What happened this afternoon? Why did you run like that?"

Because I was afraid. Of you. Of me. Of the way you made me feel. And because I know what I am. And I hate it.

"I don't have to give you an explanation—"

"But I think you do." He cupped her face in his palms, forcing her to look at him. "Why, Anna?"

She jerked free of his grasp. "Don't touch me again."

"Are you a tease? Do you enjoy arousing men and leaving them hanging? Is that it?"

"No! How dare you! How could you even suggest such a thing?"

"What alternative have you left me? What else have you given me to think of you?" She tried to turn away, he caught her arm. "Why can't you be honest with me, Annabelle?"

His fingers felt like fire on her flesh. Awareness pulsed through her. And desperation. "I ran away because I didn't want you touching me anymore. I still don't."

For long moments, he simply gazed at her. Then, slowly, deliberately, he cupped the back of her neck. "Is that so?"

"Yes," she said icily. "Now, take your hand off me. Remember, you work for me."

Rush laughed. With a flick of his fingers, he unfastened her barrette. It clattered to the floor; her hair tumbled to her shoulders. He buried his fingers in it, cupping the back of her head. He tipped her face to his, lowering his mouth until it hovered only a fraction from hers.

Anna told herself to push him away, to fight. She was such a liar; she didn't have the will to fight even for a moment. She melted against him, lifting her face to his, a whimper escaping her already parted lips.

The lights flickered, then came back on. At the same moment, Rush released her. Disoriented, Anna stumbled backward.

Rush faced her, his expression as cold and hard as ice. "You don't want me touching you, Annabelle? Tell me another one. Maybe the truth next time." He crossed the foyer, stopping when he reached the door. "But don't worry, m'lady. I won't touch you again."

Anna watched as he stepped through the door and out into the storm. She hesitated, then followed him, her heart in her throat. The urge to call him back warred with the instinct for self-preservation, leaving her indecisive and uncertain. And aching.

She raced out onto the gallery and crossed to its edge. The storm had reached its zenith, and Rush had already been swallowed in its dark fury. The rain slashed over her, soaking her to the skin; the wind tore at her hair and clothes, forcing her to place a hand on one of the columns to brace herself. But even so, she faced into the rain and wind, somehow comforted by its violence. Its life.

The places he'd touched still throbbed; her body still tingled with anticipation of his kiss. How could she feel so alive and still be so cold? she wondered, staring out at the darkness. And how could she have made such a fool of herself?

Tears welled in her eyes and slipped down her cheeks, mingling with the rain. He'd proved how much she wanted him so easily—with no more than the whisper of his breath against her mouth.

She'd whimpered and arched and clung to him.

And he hadn't even kissed her.

A fool. She was such a fool. What would a man like Rush want with her, anyway? A plain and frigid little sparrow? A woman no other man had ever wanted or loved.

It was better this way. Less confusing. Less painful. They would spend the summer repairing Ashland. No more touching and kissing. No more lemonade shared under a fragrant tree, no more fantasies. Employer and employee. Period.

Even as she made the vow to herself, she wondered if Rush was thinking of her.

Chapter Six

True to his word, Rush didn't touch her again. Nor did he mention the night of the storm or their kiss under Sweethearts' Magnolia. And as the days passed, Anna had to admit that she'd been wrong—ridiculously so.

It wasn't less confusing this way. It wasn't less painful. It was agony. She wanted to touch him, to talk to him. She couldn't stop her mind from imagining them together or remembering what it had been like in his arms.

And she couldn't stop herself from wondering if it would be different with Rush, if he would be the one man able to break through her wall of fear and insecurity and make her respond.

Anna loaded her paint roller, using the opportunity to sneak a peek at Rush. He worked on a ladder adjacent to hers, replacing weather-rotted boards on the gallery ceiling. She was following behind, sanding and painting. As he hammered the boards in place, he set his jaw in a hard, determined line, and his muscles bunched and eased with the movement.

She swallowed and dragged her gaze away. He'd put the ball in her court. All she had to do was approach him. All she had to do was be honest, tell him the truth.

A dozen times over the last couple of days she'd considered doing just that. But each time she imagined herself telling him, imagined the words passing her lips, she'd stopped herself.

Telling him wouldn't change who, or what, she was. It wouldn't make her more responsive or less afraid, wouldn't make her self-confident or attractive.

Truthfully, it wouldn't change a thing.

And she didn't think she could bear for him to look at her with pity in his eyes. Or revulsion. She'd been looked at that way before and it had hurt almost more than she'd been able to stand. And with Rush it would hurt more.

Because she wanted him more.

Rush paused to wipe the sweat from his brow. As if sensing her scrutiny, he looked at her. She flushed and went back to her paint roller, which had dripped all over the ladder and floor below while she'd been gawking at Rush.

Blue sprang from his position sprawled between the two ladders, barking ferociously. Anna looked toward the drive, lifting her hand to block the late-afternoon sun. Her brother and Travis were rounding the side of the house, heading her way.

She muttered an oath. She hadn't even heard them drive up. Just what she wasn't interested in: round one hundred and ten with her brother. Setting the roller back in the tray, she descended the ladder.

"Lowell. Travis." She inclined her head and forced a smile. "What brings you two out here?"

Her brother smiled thinly. "It always amazes me, Trav, that I need a calling card to visit my own home."

Anna gritted her teeth. She was hot, tired and on edge; the last thing she wanted to deal with was her brother's petty sarcasm. "It was just a question, Lowell."

Travis stepped forward and kissed her cheek. "I hope we haven't stopped by at an inopportune time."

"Of course not." She drew a fraction away, searching his expression for a clue to what was going on. In his she saw apology and regret, and something else she didn't recognize or know quite where to place.

"Trav?" she whispered, suddenly alarmed. "What's going on?"

Travis touched the tip of her nose with his forefinger. "Lowell just wanted to bring me out for a visit."

"Yeah," Lowell said. "Thought I'd show him around the old homestead." His lips twisted bitterly. "Trav's got a lot of good memories of this place. Certainly more than I do."

Anna sensed Rush's scrutiny and looked over her shoulder at him. He, too, had descended the ladder, and stared at her brother in open dislike and distrust.

Lowell became aware of Rush at the same moment and looked at him, arching an eyebrow in cool arrogance. "Go back to work, sis. I'll show Travis around."

After sending Anna another apologetic glance, Travis followed Lowell inside. Anna watched them go, a knot in her stomach the size of a fist. What was her brother up to? What could he be after?

"That's one class-A bastard," Rush said, coming up to stand behind her. "What's his problem?"

Anna looked over her shoulder at him. "It's complicated."

"No doubt." Rush shook his head. "Inexcusable, if you ask me."

She hadn't asked him, but she appreciated his support. It made her feel not quite so alone. She told him so.

He reached out as if to touch her, then drew his hand away. "You know, Anna, if you don't want them in the house, you don't have to allow them in."

Anna sighed, the sound defeated even to her own ears. "It isn't just my house, Rush. It's his, too."

"On paper only."

"But that's what counts, isn't it?"

Rush moved his gaze over her face, something akin to tenderness in his eyes. Anna called herself an idiot. "I could take him," he murmured. "In fact, I could take them both. Just say the word."

The sweetness of his offer rolled through her, warming places frozen by her brother's nastiness. And by her own loneliness and feelings of helplessness. She smiled. "You'd do that for me?"

He met her eyes, his crinkling at the corners. "Oh, yeah. With pleasure."

She let out a long breath, shifting her gaze to the house, wondering where Travis and Lowell were, what they were doing, if they were touching her things. She clasped her hands in front of her. "Don't think I don't appreciate it, but Lowell would only do something like sue me."

Rush shrugged and started back to the ladder. "You're the boss."

"Rush?" He stopped and looked at her, and she smiled. "Thanks."

He returned her smile. "What for? I enjoy pounding insensitive creeps."

Anna, too, went back to work. But even though she went through the motions, she couldn't put Lowell and Travis from her mind.

What were they looking at? she wondered for what seemed like the millionth time since they'd disappeared through Ashland's front doors. If Lowell was searching for another heirloom to sell, there weren't any left. Besides, Travis wouldn't stand back and allow Lowell to pull something like that. So, what were they doing?

Anna made a last sweep with the paint roller, then descended the ladder. They'd been in there at least an hour. To look at a house they both knew like the back of their hands? It didn't make any sense.

When they finally emerged, Anna had to fight to hold back a sound of relief. The sun had already begun its last dip in the west, and she and Rush had just finished cleaning up. She straightened and faced the two men as they approached.

Lowell had been drinking. She recognized the signs from years of seeing them in her father—the unnatural glint in his eyes, the swagger to his step, the mean set of his jaw. Had he found her lone bottle of chardonnay? she wondered. Or did he carry a flask these days?

Travis, looking decidedly uneasy, smiled and gave her a quick hug. The smile didn't reach his eyes. "See you soon, Anna. We'll do that dinner."

"Sure, Trav." She watched him walk to his car, then turned to her brother. "I don't know what you're looking for, Lowell. But there's nothing left for you to sell."

"No more hidden music boxes?"

Fury took her breath, and she narrowed her eyes. "That box was a gift from Mama to me. You had no right to sell it."

"A gift from Mama," he mimicked. "How sweet." He took his pack of cigarettes from his pocket and selected one. After lighting it and taking a deep drag, he met her eyes again. "Maybe I should try to sell Mama's drawings."

Anna gasped. "Don't you dare." Clenching her fingers, she took a step toward him. "You touch one of those drawings and I'll—"

Lowell laughed. "Calm down, sis. You've got your feathers all ruffled up. We both know those drawings aren't worth the paper they're drawn on."

To anyone but her. To her they were priceless. And he knew it.

She lifted her chin. "You have something to say to me, Lowell? If not, I've got things to do."

"Yeah." He smiled and drew on the cigarette again. Blowing out a long stream of smoke, he motioned to Rush with a jerk of his head. "Lose the help first."

Rush took a menacing step toward Lowell, and Anna put a restraining hand on his arm.

"You're sure, Anna?" Rush asked, eyeing Lowell with open disgust. "One punch is all it would take."

Lowell laughed, and beneath her fingers Anna felt Rush's muscles tense, readying for a fight. "I'll be fine," she murmured. "Please...could I have a moment alone with my brother?"

As soon as Rush had walked away, Lowell said loud enough for him to hear, "Slumming these days, Annabelle? You must be paying him very well."

She'd had enough. "Go to hell." She moved to brush by him and he caught her arm.

He tossed his cigarette into the grass. "I have no intentions of going anywhere just yet, sister dear."

Anna jerked her arm from his grasp and faced him. "Say your piece and go. I have no use for you anymore, Lowell."

His lips lifted in a nasty imitation of a smile. "You were wrong a moment ago, sis. There *is* something left to sell."

A shudder of unease moved over her. She fought letting it show and lifted an eyebrow with feigned cool. "Really?"

"Really." He laughed. "I'm putting my half of Ashland up for sale."

For a full ten seconds, Anna stared at him, too shocked to speak. "You can't mean it," she finally said, disbelief choking her words.

He laughed again, and the sound crawled over her nerve endings. "But I do mean it. I've offered Travis first crack at it. He's always wanted it, you know."

Anna fought to even her breathing, fought to regain her sense of equilibrium. It felt as if her whole world had been turned upside down. "But...this is my home."

"And my only asset." He narrowed his eyes. "I need the money. And I don't want Ashland."

Her own brother would do this to her. Her only family. Pain and betrayal welled inside her until she thought she might double over with it.

She met his eyes, not bothering to hide her feelings. "How could you…hurt me this way? Why do you hate me so much? What did I do to make you hate me?"

His expression softened. "I don't hate you. I hate this place. I hate my life. And I need money to change it." He reached out a hand and touched her cheek. She felt the way it trembled, and for a fraction of a moment she could believe he was still the little boy she'd loved so much. And who had loved her back.

"I'm asking a ridiculously low amount for it," he continued. "How else would I sell only half? But together, Anna, together we could get a lot more."

His words knifed through her, and she jerked away from his touch. He wasn't that little boy anymore, she reminded herself. He was a grown man, one who would stop at nothing to get his way. "How much?" she asked, flexing her fingers. "What did you offer it to Travis for?"

"Twenty-five thousand."

Twenty-five thousand! For half of their ancestral home. Their history. A laughable amount.

But more than she had a hope of coming up with.

"I'll buy you out," she said quickly. "It'll take time, but I could pay you a little every month. I could—"

"I don't want a little every month. I want it all, I *need* it all. Now." He met her eyes. In his she saw determination, and something wilder, something that bordered on frantic. "I have to have that money, Anna."

She caught his hands with her own, pleading. "Think about what you're doing, Lowell. What you're throwing away. Think—"

He jerked free of her grasp. "What do you think I've been doing? I've spent my whole life wondering how I could get away from this place. My whole life wishing..."

He bit back the thought and swung away from her. Crossing to the the gallery's edge, he stared out at the grove of magnolias. "Travis is interested. Very interested. I gave him three days to decide. Then I place ads."

First her brother. Now her oldest friend. Pain twisted inside her. How could Travis do this to her? How could he even consider her brother's offer?

Lowell turned to face her. "Let it go, Anna. Get your life back."

She shook her head. "I refuse to discuss this further."

"You avoid the future by hanging on to the past. Don't you see, Anna?" He took a step toward her, hand outstretched. "You hang on to this damn house as a way of avoiding life."

She backed away from him. "Same old story, Lowell. It's always somebody else who has a problem, always someone else who's doing something wrong. Selling Ashland isn't going to change your life. It's not going to make you like yourself more."

Lowell narrowed his eyes and took another step toward her. "No wonder Robert dumped you," he taunted. "You have passion for nothing but wood and plaster."

Anna drew in a sharp, hurt breath. His words were so painfully close to the truth. When Robert had broken their engagement he'd called her cold and unfeeling. He'd called her passionless.

Battling for control, Anna faced her brother. "Robert dumped me when he learned Daddy was dead broke and that I wouldn't be inheriting a tidy sum. He never even loved me. At the time it hurt so bad, I thought I would die. But why should you believe me? You don't think I have the capacity to feel pain."

Tears filled her eyes, choked her words. "But I do feel, Lowell. Very deeply."

"Anna, I—"

"See yourself off the property, Lowell." Turning, she went to the comfort of Ashland.

Hours later, Anna tossed aside the bedsheet and pulled herself out of bed. Although it was after midnight, she was no closer to sleep than she had been when she'd turned out the light at ten.

She should have known better than to even have tried to sleep, she thought, pulling a hand through her tousled hair. The wounds her brother had inflicted that afternoon were still too fresh to allow her rest, his threat too new to dismiss to the world of dreams.

Anna crossed to the open window. The night was clear and warm, the moon full. Its pale light fell over the plantation grounds, illuminating and shadowing, creating a dreamlike landscape, a strange and quiet kind of beauty.

Anna breathed in the night air, heavy with moisture and the scent of the night blossoms. A night for lovers, she thought. For a man and a woman, for whispered endearments and murmured promises. For kisses stolen under the pale gold moon.

For some other woman. Always some other woman.

Tears flooded her eyes. How long had it been since she'd allowed herself a romantic fantasy? How long since she'd indulged herself in a daydream?

Rush had called her a romantic that afternoon under Sweethearts' Magnolia. She supposed she had been, once upon a time. Until her dreams had been stolen from her, until the reality of life had crowded them out.

The tears slipped silently down her cheeks. She missed that girl. She missed feeling soft and warm and full of hope. Missed the feeling that someday she wouldn't be alone, that someday she would have someone to lean on and to love.

She sucked in a broken breath. And that someday she would be loved in return.

The fragrant night air tumbled through the window, drying her tears, bringing with it the songs of the cricket and bullfrog, the call of an owl, the sound of a barge out on the river. The warm, dark air beckoned her, promising comfort.

She thought of the vine-covered gazebo behind the house, of the wildflowers that grew thickly around it. And of the many dreams she had dreamed there as a girl.

Not pausing to question her own actions, she slipped on her robe and headed down the wide, curving staircase.

Within moments she was outside and heading across the lawn, the grass cool and damp against her bare feet. She had taken the path often and knew exactly where to step, which places to avoid. The gazebo stood behind the house, in the center of what had once been a lush garden. Now overgrown and tangled, more wild than manicured, the garden had the look of an uncivilized place—wild and remote.

Anna reached it, then stopped in surprise. Rush stood at the opposite edge of the gazebo, staring out at the dark fields. He didn't hear her approach, and Anna gazed at his back, not surprised to find him here. Maybe in some part of her mind, on some intuitive level, she had known he would be here and she had wanted to be with him.

She'd wanted not to be alone.

He turned and met her eyes, his shadowed. He wore as little as she: a shirt, unbuttoned, a pair of jeans that fit loose and low on his hips. His broad, muscular chest gleamed golden in the moonlight, and her pulse stirred.

A night for lovers.

"I couldn't sleep," she whispered.

"Would you like me to go?"

"No, please . . . stay."

He searched her expression, then turned back to the fields. She came up behind him, following his gaze, wondering what thoughts had kept him from sleep, wondering where the shadows in his eyes had come from.

She remembered the day they'd met, remembered thinking he hadn't told her the whole truth about his reason for being in Ames, remembered thinking that he was hiding something from her. The memory nagged at her, and she pushed it away.

"As a girl," she murmured, "I came here often. To dream my silly dreams and when . . . Daddy was in one of his moods."

Rush looked at her. "Moods?"

"Yes." Anna crossed to the bench and sat, drawing her knees up to her chest. Her bare toes peeked out from beneath the hem of her white gown and robe. "I loved my father very much, but . . . he wasn't quite stable. He retreated into these black, black moods." She met Rush's eyes. "When in those moods there was no pleasing him, no escaping his wrath."

"So you would come here."

"Mmm." She tipped her head back. Time and weather had made its mark on the gazebo, and she could see the stars through the gaping holes in its roof. "I'd fantasize about the past of Daddy's stories. I'd place myself back then in a hoop skirt and crinoline, a handsome suitor at my side."

Rush didn't smile. "You father drank, didn't he?"

Anna lowered her eyes for a moment, then lifted them back to his. "How did you know?"

Rush shrugged and came and sat beside her. "Things I heard in town."

"We Ameses, we've always been a good source of information for the gossip mill. Sometimes I wonder what they would do without us." She plucked a leaf from a vine that had wormed its way through the gazebo's lattice. "And yes, he drank. He was an alcoholic. Although I didn't realize until well past the age I should have. I was blinded by my own belief in what he was."

She looked out at the moon-cloaked fields—land that had once been Ashland's. "I didn't realize, either, that he gambled. His habits, his unhappiness, destroyed Ashland." She dropped the bit of leaf and turned her gaze back to Rush's. "I don't know why he was so unhappy. I think Mama knew, but she never spoke of it."

"Even with all his faults, you still loved him."

She lifted her hands. "How could I not? He was my father. Do you find that so hard to understand?"

"Yes. I've always judged people by their actions."

"Without emotion?"

"It's simpler that way."

She shook her head. "You can't do that with family. It's different."

Rush stood and crossed once more to the place he'd been standing when she found him. Something about his stance tugged at her heartstrings. "I wouldn't know," he said after a moment.

So that was it. Anna's heart went out to him. Even with all the trouble her family had given her over the years, even with the heartache Lowell had caused, she couldn't imagine not having a family. "You said before that you had no one. What did you mean?"

"Just what it sounds like. I have no one. I was an orphan."

"I'm sorry."

He shrugged and looked over his shoulder at her. "It's no big deal. Life throws lots of different kinds of curves. You handle it."

But it *was* a big deal, she thought. Otherwise, why would the line of his jaw be so hard, his eyes so soft and sad? She looked away, aching to murmur a word of comfort, knowing he would neither like nor appreciate the sentiment.

Silence fell between them. Clouds moved over the moon, blocking its light, and Anna shivered, thinking again of Lowell and his threat to sell half of Ashland. What would she do if she lost Ashland? Where would she go?

"Why did you come tonight?"

She looked up at him just as the clouds freed the moon, and moonlight flowed over him. Against the backdrop of the light night sky, his silhouette was broad and strong.

Anna tilted her head. Rush was a man a woman could lean on. A man whose arms were strong enough to catch her if she fell. Dangerous thoughts for a woman such as herself, she thought: a woman destined to be alone.

Tears pricked her eyes, and she blinked against them. "I came here tonight because I needed a little of the girl I used to be. Because I needed my dreams."

Emotion welled in her chest, and she laced her fingers in her lap. "Lowell dropped a bomb on me this afternoon, and I just ... needed ..."

She shook her head and looked away, unable to finish the thought.

Rush gazed at her, his chest tight. She looked so young and vulnerable, sitting there in that ruffly white gown, the moon spilling over her. A far cry from the woman who had faced him with the threat of dog and gun.

Both women stirred him. Both touched him in places and ways totally foreign to him. He should say goodnight and walk away as fast and far as possible.

He crossed to stand before her instead. He lightly touched her hair. "I'm sorry, Anna."

She looked up at him, her eyes bright with tears. Something twisted deep inside him, and he moved his hand from her hair to cup her face.

She tipped her head into the caress. "For what?"

"I'm sorry he hurt you. That he keeps on hurting you."

She drew a ragged breath. "Earlier today, you asked me what happened to turn Lowell into such a bastard. Daddy did.

"He was hard on Lowell. Disapproving. Critical. Downright cruel at times. I never understood it. Lowell was such a lovely, affectionate child. Although you'd never know it by the man he's become."

She sighed. Standing, she crossed to the edge of the gazebo and stared out at the night, lost in memories. After several moments, she looked over her shoulder at Rush. "I guess that's why I can forgive him so much."

Anna shook her head and turned back to the night. "I hated Daddy for what he did to Lowell."

Rush crossed to her, stopping directly behind her. Unable to resist, he brushed his fingers through her hair. "What of your mother, Anna? Did she just... stand back and watch?"

"Mama tried to make up to Lowell for Daddy's...dislike. She doted on him. But for some reason, he despised her for it."

Rush dropped his hands to her shoulders, gently massaging her tight muscles. Anna shuddered and eased against his chest.

"And what of you?" Rush asked. "Why does Lowell despise you?"

Anna tipped her face up to his, tears filling her eyes. "I don't know why. All I've ever done is love him." The tears brimmed over and spilled down her cheeks. "He hates Ashland, and wants to sell it. That's why he was here today." She brushed impatiently at the tears, hating her weakness. "He offered his half to Travis. For twenty-five thousand dollars."

She laughed, the sound choked with tears. "A ridiculous price. But more than I have a hope of coming up with. According to Lowell, Travis is seriously considering the offer."

"Oh, Anna... 'According to Lowell' is a big one. I think Travis wants Ashland, but not that way. And who else is going to buy half a plantation? Nobody. Half a plantation isn't any good for anything. He's just trying to maneuver you into agreeing to sell with him."

She covered her face with her hands. "I'm so tired, Rush. So damn tired of fighting."

"I know, baby." Rush turned her into his arms, his chest tight with emotion. Seeing Anna like this, vulnerable and frightened, brought out instincts in him he'd never felt before. The instinct to hold close and soothe, the instinct to slay whatever dragon necessary to protect the woman in his arms.

The emotion, the instincts, scared him silly.

But still he held her. He stroked her hair, murmuring words, sounds, of comfort.

She leaned into him. With a sigh, she slipped her arms around him and pressed her face into the crook of his neck. After a moment her tears eased, her breathing evened and she lifted her tear-streaked face up to his. "I lied to you that day you asked if I ever thought of giving up and selling Ashland. I do, Rush. Sometimes, when it's late and as dark as pitch and I'm so tired it hurts to even lay my head on the pillow, I think about it. I imagine what it would like to be free of Ashland, what it would be like to have nobody and nothing but myself to look after."

Rush brushed the tears from her cheeks. "Of course you do. You're human, Anna."

She drew in a deep, shaky breath. "Maybe I should give up. Do as Lowell wants and sell the place."

"You'd never forgive yourself." Rush smiled tenderly, moving his fingers to her soft hair, burying them in the silky strands. "You love Ashland."

"Maybe I love it too much," she whispered, tears filling her eyes once more. "Maybe Lowell's right. He says I'll always be alone because . . . I have passion for nothing but Ashland. He says—''

"No, Anna.'' Rush tipped her chin up, forcing her to look at him. "He's wrong. You're not cold, not unfeeling. He only says those things to hurt you."

She shook her head. "He does say them to hurt me, but . . . he's not wrong.''

Rush cupped her face in his palms and looked directly into her eyes. "You're a deeply passionate woman, Annabelle Ames. I see it when you look at Ashland. I feel it when you're in my arms.''

"You don't know,'' she whispered. "You don't under—''

"What don't I understand?'' He moved his hands, trailing his fingers down her throat, lightly over her collarbone. A sheen of goose bumps raced after his fingers, and she shuddered. "The way you respond to the lightest caress? The simplest touch? I understand that very well.''

Again he moved his hands, over the curve of her shoulders, down to the small of her back. She arched ever so slightly, making a small, involuntary sound of pleasure. "Or is it the way you melt against me that I don't understand? Or the way you whimper with pleasure every time I touch you?

"And what of these?'' He drew slightly away from her. The peaks of her breasts stood out in hard points, pressing against the delicate fabric of her gown and robe. He moved his hands lightly across the points, and she bit back a moan as his flesh grazed hers. "You are a deeply passionate woman.''

"I want to believe you,'' she whispered. "But I . . . know what I am.''

"Do you?" Rush cupped her bottom and drew her against him. "Do you know how much you arouse me, Annabelle? Can you feel what you're doing to me?"

Rush caught her mouth, her tongue, her strangled sounds of pleasure. She tasted of moonlight and secrets, and of her own tears. Strong and sweet and endlessly complicated, this woman moved him more than any woman ever had. She touched him in places and ways that he hadn't dreamed possible. Ways that told him she'd gotten too close, in too deep.

She would feel betrayed when she learned that he'd lied to her.

Rush moved his hands, pulling her closer. She was too vulnerable, too needy, for a man like him. A man who had nothing but passion—and the moment—to give. And she was a woman who would want everything.

But at that moment, none of that mattered worth a damn. He wanted her. In his arms, his bed.

He dragged his mouth from hers, breathing hard. "Let me show you, Anna. Let me show you how passionate you are. It would be good. Very good."

She clutched at his shoulders, her eyes dark with desire. "I want to, but I'm ... afraid."

"You tell me you're afraid, but instead I see and feel arousal."

She shook her head. "It wouldn't be... I'm not..."

"What?" Rush tightened his arms. "Just tell me, Anna. Talk to me."

She shook her head, flattening her hands against his chest. "I can't. I've got to go."

He heard the fear, the panic in her voice and searched her gaze. "Anna, what's wrong? I want you, you want me. It's simple. Natural."

A sob tore from her throat. "I wish it were.... I want so desperately..." She drew in a deep breath, obviously fighting for control. "Trust me, Rush, I'm a failure at this. I'm not any good with men. You won't be missing... a thing. Just let me go."

She pulled out of his arms; he tugged her back. "Who says you're a failure, Anna? The men you weren't interested in, the ones you turned away? Or the ones without the confidence to be gentle, the sensitivity to coax and pleasure?"

She shook her head and pushed against his chest. Rush held her tighter, forcing her to listen. "Why are you running from this? Why not face your fears head-on? The way you face everything else? You're a strong woman, Annabelle Ames. A fighter. Be honest. With me, with yourself. Whatever is between us is strong. If you decide you want to face up to it, you know where to find me."

Cupping her face in his palms, Rush pressed a quick, hard kiss to her lips, then turned and walked away.

Chapter Seven

Anna stared after Rush, the blood thrumming crazily through her veins, his words playing over in her mind.

You're a passionate woman. If you want to face up to whatever this is between us, you know where to find me.

Anna squeezed her eyes shut. She wanted to. So badly she felt as if she might die from the want. But she was afraid. Of freezing. Of once again proving to herself what a failure she was. Of disappointing Rush.

She remembered the expression in her fiancé's eyes the first time, recalled every nuance of his reaction when she'd told him about her and her past. Anna shuddered. Would Rush react the same way? She didn't think so, but she didn't think she could bear it if he did.

Anna clasped her trembling hands in front of her, wishing she could slow her frenetic heartbeat and breathe evenly. Wishing she could calmly and coolly reason with herself. But all she could think about was Rush. His hands on her body, his whispered words. *You are a deeply passionate woman, Annabelle Ames. It would be good. Very good.*

If only that were true. If only she could be sure.

She'd never felt so strongly about a man. No other man had been able to override her fears with arousal. No other had made her feel safe and womanly.

Maybe this time, she thought, pressing a hand to her chest, to her runaway heart. Maybe with this special man she would finally be a whole woman.

But what if she couldn't go through with it? What would he think of her? How would she stand it? Anna drew in a ragged breath, her head filling with the scent of flowers and warm, wet earth. If only she could be sure it would be different with Rush.

She crossed to the edge of the gazebo and the tangled path beyond. The moon had slipped behind clouds and the way was immersed in darkness. No matter how she strained to see the path's twists and turns, its low-hanging branches or pitfalls, she couldn't.

In the end all she would be able to do was trust her instincts. All she would be able to do was feel her way.

The drumbeat of her heart slowed, deepened, panic being replaced by something heavier, hotter. She couldn't be sure. She could never be sure. Unless...she tried. Unless, as Rush had said, she found the courage to face her fears.

If she didn't face them, she would never know. She would always wonder if Rush would have been the one.

Anna brought a trembling hand to her chest. She couldn't endure that. She couldn't endure a lifetime of wondering, a lifetime of what-ifs.

And her instincts told her this *was* right, that Rush was the right man.

Trust, she told herself, stepping off the gazebo and onto the darkened path. Feel the way.

Anna moved down the tangled, wild path, walking at first, then running. Suddenly, every moment of not knowing, of not being with Rush, seemed an eternity of agony. She had to be with him. She had to know.

Branches caught at her gown; she heard the fabric rip. She stepped on something hard and sharp; she didn't pause. Several times she stumbled, but she righted herself and kept on running.

She had to get to Rush; she had to know.

As she cleared the path just before the overseer's house, the moon broke free of the clouds, illuminating the way, bathing her in its soft but brilliant light. She ran up the cottage steps and let herself inside.

Moonlight streamed through the unadorned windows, painting the interior in pale gold. She found her way easily into the hall, to the first bedroom. The door stood ajar. With the tips of her fingers she pushed it the rest of the way open.

Rush waited for her by the window, backlit by the moon. Anna was struck again by the strength of his silhouette, and by his rugged good looks. She sucked in a quick breath. He was the man she'd always dreamed of.

Rush turned. Their eyes met. He didn't speak, but his gaze seemed to ask if she was sure.

She'd never been so sure of anything.

"I'm glad you came," he murmured, moving toward her.

She clasped her hands in front of her, fighting for an even breath. "Me, too," she whispered.

He caught her hands and rubbed them between his. "They're so cold."

"I'm so afraid."

"I know." He brought her hands to his mouth, pressing a kiss to each of her palms. "I'll be very careful," he murmured. "Very gentle."

At his touch, tongues of flame licked at the edges of her fear. "I'm afraid I'm going to... disappoint you."

"You won't." He drew her farther into the room, stopping when they stood in a patch of the pale gold moonlight.

"But I might..." She worked to form the words. "I might freeze."

"If you do, we'll work through it." He trailed his mouth over her cheeks, to her forehead, her eyelids. "I promise, Anna. We'll work through it."

He seemed unsurprised and unruffled by her admission. Her fear ebbed a fraction more. She shuddered and melted against him. "Thank you," she whispered. "Thank you so much."

Her humble words tore at him. What kind of men had she known in the past? Who had treated her with such an absence of care that she thought so little of herself?

He drew away from her and met her eyes. "Do you think I'm so selfless, Anna? Do you think I'm not getting something wonderful from this?"

He could tell from her expression that she didn't, and he muttered an oath. "I want you so much I can't sleep. Can't concentrate." He pushed the robe from her shoulders. It floated to the floor like a cloud. "I haven't been able to do much of anything except fantasize about you in my arms, naked in my bed."

He moved his fingers rhythmically against her exposed shoulders, gentling her, reassuring her. Beneath his fingers, Rush felt her muscles loosening, then liquifying. Anna tilted her head, a small sigh of pleasure slipping past her lips.

He took the opportunity to press a kiss to her warm, satiny throat. The skin there was as soft and white as a magnolia petal, as fragrant as the entire blossom. The scent, at once sweet and potent, filled his head.

"Remember the morning I looked up and saw you standing on the gallery?" he asked against her ear. "You were wearing this gown. It revealed nothing, yet I needed a cold shower that morning and a dozen more since then." He lowered his voice to a husky whisper. "I should be thanking you, my sweet. I despise cold showers."

Anna laughed, the sound delicate but full of pure female satisfaction. The sound warmed him, deeply and in a way he'd never experienced before. Cupping her face, Rush caught her mouth in a lingering kiss.

When he ended the kiss, she opened her eyes. They stared at one another for long moments. "You're trusting me with your fears, Anna. With your beautiful body. That's a gift. One to be treasured. I will treasure it. I promise."

Anna's heart tipped over. No one had ever said such things to her before; no one had ever made her feel special, desirable. And for the first time in her life, she believed she was. For the first time in her life, it felt right, so right, to be with a man.

"Oh, Rush..." Anna drew his head down to hers and caught his mouth, pouring out her appreciation for the man he was, her wonder at the way he made her feel.

At her arousal.

It throbbed through her, warming places that had once been cool, awakening places that had slumbered, dampening places that had once been arid. She clung to him as they kissed, one long, drugging exchange after another.

Through the thin fabric of the gown, she felt the rapid rise and fall of his chest, felt the thunder of his heart. And she felt his arousal. Hard and insistent, it pressed against her, at once exciting and frightening.

Anna drew in a quick breath, her heart beginning to beat unnaturally fast. As if sensing her fears, he murmured sounds of comfort and moved a fraction away from her, giving her space, letting her know that as promised, he would cherish her.

Softly, slowly, Rush moved his hands over her body. His muscles quivered with the effort of holding his passion in check, with the effort it took to keep from tumbling her to the bed and making passionate, demanding love to her.

Instead, he eased her carefully onto the mattress and peeled away her gown. In the moonlight her body gleamed smooth and white and womanly. He moved the flat of his hands ever-so-lightly over her curves, delighting in the way she shuddered and quivered at his touch.

How had he ever thought her plain? he wondered, struck by her beauty. How had he ever thought her sturdy? She was lithe and delicate, her body finely honed from years of physical work. Her breasts were firm, her nipples the color of just ripe strawberries. He took one into his mouth, stroking with his tongue, then gently nipping.

Annabelle arched and cried out. She clutched at him. What was happening to her? she wondered dizzily. She'd never felt this way before, never even imagined she could. She closed her eyes, totally attuned to her body, to her reactions, to Rush's touch.

As he moved his mouth from her breast, her breath shuddered past her lips, leaving her empty until he caught the other one. She filled her lungs again, suspended on an imaginary plane of pure pleasure.

She moved beneath him, rotating her hips in an instinctual invitation. She burned for him to touch her in other, more secret places. She burned to have him inside her.

"Rush...please. I..."

"Okay, baby...hold on." He laced his fingers with hers, catching her mouth once more, this time urgently. He kissed her deeply, his skin growing almost unbearably hot under her fingers, the breath heaving from his lungs. Moving fully over her, Rush positioned himself between her legs, his arousal pushing and probing against her.

Anna stiffened as fear washed over her. It stole her arousal; it mocked her for her ridiculous hopes. With the fear came disappointment, cold and bitter and biting.

Anna squeezed her eyes shut and told herself to relax. She worked to find her arousal again, to tune in to the sensations that a moment ago had had her burning to be one with Rush.

They were gone. Extinguished like the flame of a candle in a wind. Anna bit back a cry of frustration and disappointment. She'd been so certain Rush was the one. So certain that...this time she would...

"Anna?" Rush eased off her. "Baby, what's wrong?"

"I can't do this," she whispered, squeezing her eyes more tightly shut in an attempt to ward off tears. They slipped from them anyway and rolled hotly down her cheeks. "I'm sorry, Rush, I...just...I can't—"

"Shh. It's okay." He drew away from her, until he lay on his side just beyond her, propped up on an elbow.

She turned her face from his. "I'm so embarrassed."

"Don't be." With his forefinger, he tipped her face gently back to his. "You've done nothing to embarrass yourself."

"But I... You..." She caught her bottom lip between her teeth. "This is awful and awkward."

"Only if you make it so." Rush sifted his fingers through her silky hair, fanned out across his pillow.

She looked up at the ceiling, her vision blurred by tears. "What happened in your life to make you so wonderful?"

"Me? Wonderful?" He arched his eyebrows in mock disbelief. "I don't think I've ever been called that before." One corner of his mouth lifted in amusement. "Now 'jerk,' that's a different story."

She shook her head, her tensed muscles beginning to ease. "Uh-uh. I've been with jerks before."

"You want to tell me about it?"

She hesitated. She did want to tell him; she wanted him to really know her. Needed him to. Her heart began to pound, the old familiar fears and what-ifs pressing in on her.

She began to shake. Rush must have felt it, but he didn't comment. Instead he curved an arm protectively around her.

"You don't have to, Anna."

Again she thought of taking the coward's way. But she couldn't, she realized. She wouldn't be able to live with herself if she did. She shook her head. "I want to tell you."

"Okay." He looked into her eyes. "I promise I'll be careful with you. You can tell me anything. I won't judge."

But would he be repulsed, as Robert had been? Or embarrassed and shamed, as her mother had been?

It didn't matter. She hadn't the ability to either guess his reaction or change it. Telling him was something she wanted to do for herself.

So she did. Simply. Baldly.

"I was raped when I was fifteen."

She felt Rush stiffen, heard his tightly drawn breath. But he didn't move away from her, didn't try to avoid her eyes when she looked at him. "His name was Lee and he was a couple of years older than me."

Anna swallowed and shifted her gaze once again to the ceiling, hurtled back to that awful summer day. "His daddy and mine were friends. Sometimes Lee would come over with his father." She shook her head, lost in the memory. "I had such a big crush on him. I remember spending hours thinking about him, praying that he'd stop by.

"One day when he did, he asked me to go for a walk. I was ecstatic. We walked out into the fields, talking, holding hands. I was so happy because I thought he . . . liked me."

Rush muttered an oath and tightened his arm around her.

"Anyway, when we were way out in the fields he started kissing me and...touching me. He was moving too fast and I got scared. I'd never done anything with a boy but kiss. When I tried to push him away he got rough. And angry. He called me terrible names. He slapped me."

Anna fought to control the tears choking her words, blinding her. "Then, when I tried to run, he pushed me down and...forced himself...inside me. I pleaded with him to...stop, but he...wouldn't."

"One of the worst parts was, Macy started calling for me. I could hear her, could hear the concern in her call. But she...couldn't help me. Lee had his hand over my mouth and..."

Unable to hold back her tears, Anna turned and pressed her face into Rush's chest. "After...he just...walked...away."

Rush wrapped his arms around her, drawing her tightly against him. "Oh, baby, it's over now. That boy can't hurt you anymore. And if anyone else tries, I'll kill them. I promise I will."

He held her as she sobbed, stroking her hair and back, murmuring sounds of comfort. After a while her tears eased and she lay quietly against his side.

"What happened to him, Anna?" he asked, moving his fingers in slow circles at the small of her back. "Was he arrested?"

She shook her head. "No. I didn't even tell anyone for a couple of weeks. I was so...ashamed. I thought I'd done something...wrong. I thought that somehow I'd...invited his—"

"His violence?" Rush said, his voice tight.

"Yes." Anna drew in a deep breath, careful not to meet his eyes, afraid suddenly of what she might see in them. "Anyway, Macy came upon me in the gazebo one afternoon a couple of weeks later and I was...crying. She asked me what was wrong. And I told her."

"Oh, baby." Rush pressed his lips to the top of her head. "Poor baby."

"I begged her not to tell Mama or Daddy, but she insisted. Mama was...shocked. Dismayed. They decided it would be best if they said nothing. They were worried about my reputation."

"Your reputation!" Rush exploded. "What about punishing that bastard for what he did to you?"

Anna flattened her hands on Rush's chest. She felt his anger, in the wild thud of his heart, in his taut muscles. She heard the outrage in his voice.

He didn't blame her. He wasn't repulsed, wasn't so discomfited that he couldn't face her.

Tears welled in her eyes again, and she squeezed them shut. "So much time had passed and...it was his word against mine. They were afraid—"

"Nobody would believe you."

"Yes. And then everybody would know I was...spoiled." Again Rush swore, and this time it was Anna who stroked and soothed. "We never told Daddy. They were afraid of his reaction, afraid that when he was in one of his moods, something terrible would happen. But Macy told her husband Brady."

Anna shifted her gaze away from Rush's. "A couple weeks after she did, Lee got beat up. Real bad. He was almost killed. Rumor was a gang of militant blacks from over in Bolivar County did it. Which made sense because Lee was a racist. He was always saying and doing terrible things to blacks. Inquiries were made, but nothing ever came of it.''

''You think Macy's husband arranged it?''

''I know he did. And maybe you'll think I'm an awful person, but I felt so good after. I felt like I... mattered to somebody. I felt like somebody cared about what had happened to me.''

''I care,'' Rush whispered. ''I wish I could do... something to make it better for you.''

''You already have,'' she said simply. ''You listened. You didn't judge.''

He tipped her face up to his. ''You're a special woman, Annabelle Ames. And I'm going to kiss you. Now.'' He caught her mouth, softly at first, then pressing, delving deeper. He tasted the salt of her tears, the sweetness of her response. Parting her lips, he found her tongue, toying with it at first, then stroking deeply.

Her story had angered him in an almost primal way. He'd had to fight the urge to find this boy and punish him himself. It had taken a shocking amount of control to continue to quietly listen and reassure her. But he had, because that's what Anna had needed.

Now she needed to be loved. Now she needed to know how wonderful it could be between a man and a woman. She needed to know passion.

He would show her.

If he could hold himself back long enough. He wanted her with a ferocity that stunned him, a ferocity he couldn't remember experiencing before, though he must have. For if he hadn't, this woman would be truly special, this experience extraordinary. And he couldn't have that. He couldn't have become that involved with her.

He would try to remember later, to reassure himself, but for now there was only Anna—her soft, thick hair and even softer mouth, the way she moved and whimpered under his touch, her pain and her passion.

He pressed her back into the mattress and tangled his fingers in her hair. "Look at me, Anna." She opened her eyes; they were heavy-lidded and dark with awareness. "You're so beautiful," he murmured. "So exciting."

She smiled tremulously, and his heart wrenched. "You don't have to say that to me. It doesn't—"

"I don't say things I don't mean." Rush moved his fingers over her high cheekbones, down the line of her fine, straight nose, along the contour of her soft, full mouth. "You are beautiful, Anna. And passionate." He smiled. "Get ready, babe, because now I'm going to show you just how passionate."

He caught her to him, finding her mouth, her tongue. He moved his hands over her body, igniting fires with his fingers, arousing her to a fever pitch. One moment he moved with excruciating slowness, the next he rushed, plunging her headlong into a maelstrom of response.

She forgot her fear, lost track of all the times and ways she had failed in the past. Sensation took the place of fear. And with it, need. Sweet and biting, all-consuming.

Anna pulled him to her, onto her, trembling now with urgency—to feel his flesh pressed against hers. She roamed her hands over him, exploring, learning. Reveling in the hard, angular feel of him against her palms.

She felt his passion—and his control—in the quivering of his muscles. Under her hands his skin grew damp and hot. She grew bolder at this evidence of her effect on him, and let her mouth explore the places her hands already had.

How could she fear freezing again when her body was consumed by heat? she wondered. Places she hadn't even known existed pulsed with awareness, throbbed with a primal, instinctual rhythm.

Rush dragged her mouth back up to his. Anna drew in a ragged, sobbing breath. She wanted something, needed something that was just beyond her reach. It built inside her, and she moved her hips against his, whimpering his name.

Rush murmured something low and urgent. He found her with his fingers, and buried himself inside her. She arched and cried out, clutching at the bedding.

"That's right, sweetheart," he whispered, stroking. "Let go and enjoy." His fingers continued their rhythmic magic, even as he caught the tip of one breast in his mouth.

Anna cried out his name, bucking against his hand, reaching up for a blinding star and catching it. The star exploded in her head, and she fell back against the bed, sobbing.

Rush was there, holding her, stroking her face and hair. "There, baby. Go ahead and cry. Let it out."

She clutched at him, feeling strange and miraculous and new. And free. Free for the first time since she was fifteen years old.

And at almost forty, she was finally a woman.

Anna tilted her face to his, searching his expression. She wanted to tell him what he'd done for her, what this meant to her, but as she started to form the words, she realized how they would sound. Smitten. Adoring. Lovestruck, even.

And Rush was a man who would run from such flowery emotion. She didn't know how she knew, but she did.

"You're tired, sweet." Rush smiled softly and pushed the dampened tendrils of hair away from her face. "Go ahead and get some rest."

"But..." She looked up at him, feeling herself flushing wildly. "But you didn't...you know."

He smiled again and pressed a quick kiss to her lips. "It doesn't matter."

"But you... That's not...fair." She sounded like a high-school girl, and blushed again. "I do know how these things work."

Rush laughed and hugged her. "I'll survive, Anna. I promise."

"I know. But I...want to make you as happy as you made me."

His smile faded and he gazed at her, a strange expression on his face. One that made her sad. "Rush, I didn't mean to—"

He touched his forefinger to her mouth, silencing her. "I had pleasure. Don't you know how exciting it was to watch you?" He ran the flat of his hand over her damp abdomen. "How exciting to know I was your first?"

At her look he smiled. "I *was* your first. Nobody else counted, because nobody else has ever made you...sing. Besides," he finished wickedly, "we have the whole summer."

But she didn't want to leave it this way, Anna thought. She wanted to make him as happy as he'd made her, give him as much pleasure. And by doing so she could tell him without words what being with him had meant to her—what he meant to her.

"No," she whispered, her voice a throaty imitation of her own. "You're not getting out of this so easily."

With a boldness she'd been incapable of only minutes ago, she found him. He made a sound of pleasure and swelled under her fingers. She flushed, feeling powerful and womanly.

"Anna, do you know what—"

"Yes . . . I do." She moved her hand again, slowly, rhythmically. "I want to do this, Rush. I want to make love with you. Please . . . guide me."

He had neither the will nor the want to deny her, and drew her into his arms. They began again, kissing, stroking, exploring. Only this time Anna knew what waited at the end. This time she had no fear. Only arousal. Only anticipation.

When the time came, Rush slipped into her slowly, taking care not to hurt her, not to frighten her. She stiffened but for only a moment, then a shudder moved over her and she wrapped her legs around his.

Rush told himself to hold back; he tried to remember how she'd been frightened, how she'd been hurt. But the feel of her wrapped around him made careful and cautious an impossibility. With a muttered cry, Rush caught her mouth.

They rocked together, slowly at first, building to a crescendo. Anna dug her fingers into his shoulders; his mouth caught her cry of pleasure.

As hers caught his.

For a long time after they lay twined together, the sheets a damp tangle around them. Moonlight and the warm night air tumbled through the window, bringing with it the faint scent of the magnolias.

Anna sighed and snuggled against him, her heart full to bursting. She'd never imagined being with a man could be like this, even in her wildest fantasies. And she'd never felt so special, so cherished.

Her cheeks heated. She couldn't start thinking this was more than it was, she warned herself. Rush was a drifter. He was leaving after the summer.

He had promised her nothing.

"Happy?" he asked quietly.

That he should ask that question now was painfully ironic. She lifted her face to his and smiled anyway. Tomorrow could take care of itself. "Yes. Deliriously so."

"Deliriously?" he teased. "I *am* good."

"Conceited," she countered, tracing lazy figure eights on his stomach. "And terribly arrogant."

"Is that so?"

"I should have fired you when I had the chance."

He yawned. "Yeah, but then you wouldn't have had the opportunity to mess around with the hired help."

"Good point." She moved her fingers to his chest. "Rush?"

"Hmm?"

"Do we have to go to sleep?"

He arched an eyebrow. "You have a better suggestion?"

She did. Inching up, she whispered it in his ear. "What do you think?"

He pulled her to him. "I think you might kill me before the end of the summer." He lowered his mouth until it hovered a fraction above hers and grinned wickedly. "But what the hell? A guy has to go sometime."

Chapter Eight

Rush sat bolt upright in bed, heart pounding, skin slick with sweat. Moonlight spilled through the windows, helping to dispel the shadows of his dreams. He rubbed his hands over his face, shocked to see that they shook.

The shadows hadn't visited him since he'd come to Ashland. Until tonight. Until after he'd made love with Annabelle.

He swore softly and gazed down at her. She slept peacefully, her breathing deep and undisturbed. What did it mean that the shadows had visited him tonight? Nothing? Probably. But nonetheless his psyche's timing sucked. Big time.

Rush dragged his hands through his hair, still feeling the effects of the dream; feeling the frustration, the sense of emptiness and loss. The dream never varied.

In it he was searching, reaching out to shadowy images always just beyond his grasp.

He didn't need a shrink to explain what his subconscious was telling him tonight—he needed to remember the reason why he'd come to Ashland.

He checked the bedside clock, only two hours till dawn.

And only two hours since he'd last made love with Anna.

Rush lowered his gaze to her face, unbearably soft in sleep. With his forefinger, he touched the curve of her cheek. Her skin was flushed, warm against his fingertip. He could make love to her again, he realized. This very moment. Just looking at her stirred him.

What an experience making love with her had been. Exciting and erotic. Passionate and totally fulfilling. And tender. In a way lovemaking never had been for him before.

Rush drew his hand away from her cheek, discomfited by the realization. He shouldn't have given in to his attraction to her; they shouldn't have made love. She would want something from him that he couldn't give.

Rush slipped quietly out of bed. Not bothering to dress, he went out to the front porch and the warm, black night.

Leaning against one of the rough-hewn columns, he stared up at the inky sky. What the hell was he doing here? Certainly not what he'd come to do. He made a sound of self-disgust. After the first round of inquiries, he'd made no progress at all. He hadn't even been into town in a week.

He'd been too busy becoming involved with Annabelle.

Dammit. He rubbed his hand along his stubbled jaw. He'd created an impossible situation. Already, he knew, she hoped he would stay. Already, she cared too much for him.

Anna put down roots. It was her way. He'd known that about her from the beginning.

He'd never had roots. He never would. That was his way. Only he doubted she understood him as well as he did her.

He would hurt her.

Even as he'd drawn her onto the bed with him he had understood the ramifications of his actions. Yet he'd been unable to stop himself. She'd called to him so deeply and so strongly, he'd been unable to leave her alone... or deny himself.

Rush turned his gaze to Ashland. It rose, monument-like, out of the darkness. A symbol of history and constancy. A symbol of both the ephemeral quality of life and of permanence.

A symbol of everything he would never be.

He wasn't posing as a drifter, Rush realized. He was one. He'd dropped everything in his life to come here. Without one hitch. No family. No friends. No romantic ties. Even his business functioned without him.

He'd long ago cut himself off from the world of people and emotions. Yet something about Ashland—about Anna—made him think about the things he'd given up. Made him long for them.

Rush fisted his fingers. He refused to long for anything, refused to feel the great gaping place inside him—the place that yearned for something always just beyond his grasp. He'd closed himself to it long ago. He'd learned that he functioned best without people. Without messy emotional ties or commitments.

Rush frowned. He shouldn't have started this affair with Anna.

He had to end it.

"What's wrong?"

He turned. Anna stood in the doorway, clutching a blanket to her chest. Her eyes were soft with sleep, her expression heartbreakingly vulnerable.

His own heart tipped over. She needed him. In a way he'd never been needed before. In a way that scared him senseless.

Even as he told himself to make a clean break now, he smiled reassuringly. "Nothing's wrong. I'm a light sleeper. That's all."

She didn't believe him; he could tell by the wounded look in her eyes. And by the way she hesitated in the doorway, like a frightened bird preparing for flight.

"I don't regret our having made love," he said softly, realizing as he uttered the words that despite everything, he spoke the truth. He didn't regret; maybe tomorrow or the next day he would, but not now. "If that's what you're thinking, stop it right now."

"I know that I was..." She inched her chin up, just a fraction, as if preparing herself for a blow. "It was probably...disappointing for you."

"Hardly." Rush crossed to where she stood and cupped her face in his palms. "Annabelle, my sweet, it doesn't get any better than that."

Her lips curved into a shy but brilliant smile. At its sweetness, a lump formed in his throat. Messy, he thought. He was in so far and so deep already, he might never be able to dig himself out.

And at this moment he had neither the fortitude nor strength of will to even try.

"Really?" she asked.

"Really." He pressed his mouth to hers. "Unless, of course, I was the one who disappointed?"

She blushed crimson and shook her head. "No way."

Charmed, Rush laughed softly and drew her with him to the edge of the porch. There, he unwound her blanket and slipped inside, folding it around them both. Anna sighed and snuggled into his side.

It was warm under the blanket. Her curves molded to his planes, her flesh to his, and awareness rippled through him. How was it possible that he wanted her again—so soon and so strongly? What was it about this woman that turned him inside out and upside down?

He ran the flat of his hand over her hip, pleased when she didn't stiffen or flinch. She'd grown accustomed to his touch already. She trusted him.

Uncomfortable, Rush drew her closer to his side and for long moments, they stared out at Ashland.

"It's such a beautiful night," she whispered.

"But it's almost morning."

"Yes." She sighed again and tilted her face up to his. "I don't remember the last time I've seen so many stars."

"The sky's never like this in Boston. Too many lights, too much pollution."

As they gazed up at the heavens, a star shot across it. Anna caught her breath and squeezed her eyes shut. When she opened them, her cheeks were bright with color. "Macy says that stars are really angels, and when you see a shooting star it's an angel rushing to see God. That's why if you make a wish on a shooting star, it always comes true."

Rush turned her to him. "Always?"

"Mmm-hmm."

"And what did you wish for, Annabelle Ames?"

The color in her cheeks deepened, and she shook her head. "Macy says if you tell, it won't come true."

"And Macy's word is gospel?"

"Definitely. In many ways she was more a mother to me than my own mother was."

Rush drew his eyebrows together. "Wasn't Macy the woman I met the other day?"

"Mmm-hmm. She was the housekeeper at Ashland the whole time I was growing up. And self-imposed nanny." Anna smoothed her hand over Rush's chest and flat belly. "She and her husband lived here, in this cottage."

The overseer and his wife were black, Rush realized with a shock. He'd never even considered that. He sucked in a sharp breath, disappointment spearing through him. He couldn't be their son, or any other blood relation of theirs.

Yet nothing else in Ames stirred his memory. Nothing but Ashland and this overseer's house. He'd been so certain—in his gut—that the overseer and his wife were the keys to his past.

Another theory shot to hell.

"Rush?" Anna tipped her face up to his. "What happened to your family?"

He looked at her in surprise. It was as if she'd read his thoughts. "Why do you ask?"

"You said you were an orphan. I just wondered...what happened to your parents and the rest of your family."

"Actually, I don't know what happened." He frowned, shifting his gaze to the horizon. "I was delivered to an orphanage at age five. I don't know by whom. I might have family somewhere."

"Would you like to find them?"

Rush looked at her, his expression hard. "I'd like to know who I am. There's a difference."

Anna lifted a hand to his cheek and stroked it gently. "I'm sorry. I shouldn't have asked. I—"

"Don't worry about it," he said harshly. "I don't."

But he did. She saw it in the haunted look in his eyes, in the hard line of his jaw. She caught his hand and brought it to her mouth.

She hated to see him this way, hated that she'd ruined the mood with her careless question.

She turned so she completely faced him and folded her arms around his waist. She kissed his shoulders, his chest, trailing her tongue and mouth across his flesh, delighting in the sounds of pleasure he made, in the way he grew absolutely still as if absorbing her touch.

She wanted to comfort him as he'd comforted her earlier. She wanted to let him know, in a way that he would accept, that she cared for him; that she thought he was special and wonderful.

She caught his right nipple, nipping it, drawing it into a tight pebble with her tongue. She moved to his left one, pleasuring it, and him, again.

She dropped to her knees. The blanket slipped to the floor. She dipped her tongue into the indentation of his belly button, then moved lower still.

With a groan, Rush followed her down, tumbling her back against the blanket. He caught her mouth and plunged into her just as the sun peeked over the horizon, shooting colored light across the sky.

Hours later, Anna gazed at Rush. The night before had the quality of a bizarre, erotic dream. They'd made love so many times, with the last being almost unreal in its perfection.

And yet, through it all she'd been unable to stop thinking of what he'd said about his past; had been unable to forget the tone of his voice, the expression in his eyes.

"I was delivered to an orphanage at age five...."

"I'd like to know who I am, Anna. There's a difference."

Those words had stayed with her the rest of the night, intruding on her sleep, invading her dreams. Why did she have the feeling that his wanting to know who he was had something to do with her? How could it?

Because his feelings for himself had everything to do with his feelings for her.

She frowned. She wished that weren't true. She wished she didn't feel it to be true deep down in her gut.

There had been something ferocious about the way Rush had loved her that last time. There'd been a desperation in the way he had touched her. It had frightened her. Not as she used to be frightened—of being hurt or freezing—but in a way that cut closer to her heart.

It was almost as if he'd already said goodbye.

Nonsense. She shook her head. They had the whole summer ahead of them. He'd said so. She was an innocent in the ways of lovemaking, that was all. She didn't understand passion's various forms or subtleties.

Not yet, anyway. She would soon.

Propping herself on an elbow, she gazed down at him. She smiled, thinking of the days and nights ahead. It seemed an endless collection of hours to . . . learn; to make love.

Her cheeks burned. How much she'd changed in the space of eight hours! How much Rush had changed her!

Her smile faded. But it wasn't an endless amount of time. In the space of her life, it was so fleeting as to be almost nonexistent.

How many days? she wondered, counting in her head. June was already drawing to a close. The end of August she started back to school. Two months. Only two months.

And then he would be gone.

She'd fallen in love with him.

Her heart leapt to her throat. No, she couldn't have. Forty-year-old Southern spinsters didn't fall in love with handsome Yankee drifters.

She clutched at the bedding, a feeling akin to panic coursing through her. She knew so little about him, so little about his life. He had secrets.

She wasn't reckless, she wasn't foolhardy.

But she was in love with him.

Anna moved her gaze over his face, boyish in sleep. What more did she need to know about him? He was kind and patient. Honest and gentle. The kind of man who could take a frightened and frigid woman and make her . . . sing.

He was the man she'd always dreamed of.

Wonder filled her. It felt good to love. To trust. To know she could put her body in the hands of this man without fear. He wouldn't judge. He would never deride her, never laugh. Never hurt her.

She'd never felt this way before.

Smiling softly, she reached out and gently touched his mouth. He stirred sleepily and twitched his nose. Biting back a girlish and delighted giggle, she plucked a feather from one of the pillows and trailed it across his eyelids, around the shell of his ear, down his nose.

His nose twitched again, and this time she didn't catch the giggle in time. But still, he didn't awaken.

She grew bolder. She leaned closer. His hand shot out and caught hers. "I wouldn't," he muttered, not opening his eyes.

"No?" She tickled the corner of his mouth with the bit of down. "And why no—"

Before she could finish the question, he'd tumbled her against his chest, then flipped her onto her back. He lay across her, pinning her to the mattress. At her sputter of surprise, he laughed. "That's why."

His eyes were clear, unshadowed by sleep. She narrowed her own eyes. "How long have you been awake?"

He laughed. "I'll never tell."

She slipped her arms around his neck and laced her fingers together. "Pretending to be asleep is in very poor taste."

His smile widened. "So is ogling, then tickling your bed partner when he's asleep and unable to defend himself."

"I certainly was not ogling."

"Really? What do you call it down here, perusing the goods?"

"Indeed not." She sniffed haughtily. "Really, you drive me crazy."

He nuzzled the side of her neck. "I try."

"Mmm..." She arched as he skimmed his hands over the sides of her breasts. "I've got an idea."

"Does it involve you naked?"

She blushed. "No."

"Shucks," he drawled wickedly. "And there you'd gone and gotten my hopes up." Catching her hand, he brought it to him.

Her eyes widened. "Not already?"

"I told you how much I wanted you."

His breath caught as her fingers circled him. His body responded forcefully and she laughed, delighted with her own power. "And you said *I* was going to kill *you*."

"Vixen."

"Don't you want to hear my idea?"

"Later," he muttered, lowering his mouth to hers. "Because now I have some ideas of my own."

"Take the day off?" Rush repeated, lifting his eyebrows in feigned shock. "Don't you think that's a bit radical, Ms. Ames?"

"It is Saturday." She scooted off the bed and slipped her gown quickly over her head. "And I don't feel like working."

"Then come back here."

He grabbed for her; she dodged his grasp and pulled on her robe. "Oh, no. Blue's probably eaten the sofa by now, and I can hardly walk as it is."

He wiggled his eyebrows. "I could massage those aching muscles. Of course, that's what made you sore in the first place." She blushed wildly, and he laughed and climbed out of bed. "Oh, all right. But what's the use of taking a day off if—"

The phone rang.

Rush stopped in his tracks but didn't make a move toward it. Anna laughed. "Aren't you going to answer it?"

"Probably a wrong number."

It rang again, then again. She shook her head and started for the door. "Go ahead and get it. I'll go tend to Blue." She stopped at the door and met his eyes. "If you hurry, you might be able to catch me in the shower."

Rush dove for the phone, picking it up to the sound of Anna's laughter and the screen door slapping shut.

"Rush Cousins?"

"It is." Rush dragged his attention to the caller.

"This is Dr. Pete Garner. I'm sorry it's taken me so long to get back to you. I've been out of town."

The local G.P., Rush thought. Son of the man who had been the local doctor the year he was born. Finally.

"My receptionist tells me you're trying to get some information about the birth of a boy child in 1949 or 1950?"

"That's right."

"Do you mind telling me why you're interested?"

Rush hesitated, then quickly filled him in, leaving out all reference to Ashland Plantation and the music box. "I would appreciate it if you could keep this information confidential. At least for the time being. Small towns have active tongues."

"And long memories," the doctor supplied. "Memories that might be of some help."

"I'd still like to keep it under wraps for a while, if you don't mind."

The doctor was silent for a long moment. "You say you have a strong reason for believing you were born in Ames?"

Rush thought of his reaction to the music box, and of the strange little woman who had sold it to him. "Yes," he said firmly.

"You've already been down to city hall and looked through the birth registry?"

"Yes. There wasn't one Cousins listed. I've also checked microfilm issues of the Ames *Gazette* from 1949 for news of births, deaths and local gossip. Nothing."

"It is intriguing," the doctor murmured. "But how can I help?"

"I understand your father was the only doctor around back then, and I thought maybe there would be something in his old files. If you still have them."

"I do. And you do understand correctly. For years my daddy was the only medical care available in the entire county. And beyond, really."

"So if there are any medical records to be found, you'd have them."

"Yes, but…medical information is confidential. I'd really like to help you, but—"

"Look," Rush inserted quickly, "I'm not trying to find my family. I don't plan to approach anyone. All I'm trying to do is find out who I am. I just want to know where I come from."

Rush could almost hear the man on the other end thinking, weighing his answer. Rush tried to give him another nudge. "Surely a lot of those files are inactive. The information I'm looking for is over forty years old."

The doctor made a sound of reluctant acquiescence. "Okay. Give me a couple of hours to pick through the files. I'll see what I can find."

Rush let out a relieved breath. "Thanks, Doc. I appreciate it."

After getting directions and finalizing a time for him to stop by the office, Rush hung up the phone, his heart thundering against the wall of his chest. This could be it. This could lead to something.

What the hell was he going to tell Anna?

The truth.

Rush balled his hands into fists. Dammit, he didn't want to. Even though she deserved to know. Even though he should have told her long ago.

She would be angry, hurt.

He needed her help. She would know the people to talk to, who the old-timers were. She might even know about him. His mystery would be solved and he could go home.

His gut twisted at the thought of leaving Ashland. Of leaving Anna. It would hurt. Hurt in a way he hadn't in so long, he couldn't remember when.

Rush shook his head. He would tell her tonight, after he'd talked to Dr. Garner. He would bring her the music box. It belonged at Ashland; it belonged with Anna.

And maybe it would help her to forgive him.

He showered quickly, then dressed and headed for the plantation house. The scent of bacon and eggs led him to Anna. She stood at the stove, Blue at her feet. She smiled at him when he walked into the kitchen, and guilt washed over him.

He stooped and scratched Blue's ears, unable to meet Anna's eyes.

"Guess you decided against a shower," she said, setting the filled plates on the table.

He saw that her hands shook, and he swore silently. He'd hurt her already. "I figured I'd missed my opportunity. The call took longer than I expected."

She poured them both a cup of coffee. "Oh?"

He didn't reply to the question in her voice. "It smells great."

"Have a seat."

They both sat. Rush took a bite of his eggs. "Delicious."

"Thanks." She pushed her own eggs around the plate.

He cleared his throat. "I've got to go into town. I've an errand to run."

She looked up. "I'll come, too. There are some things I need from the drugstore."

"I'll pick them up for you. Just give me a list."

She gazed at him a moment, then stood and took her untouched food to the sink. Blue whined and she handed the dog her piece of toast, then scraped the rest into the trash.

That done, she turned and faced him. Gone was the hurt he'd seen in her eyes only moments ago. Now she looked indignant. And angry.

"Are you married?"

The question took him so by surprise, he nearly choked. "Annabelle, where did that come fro—"

"Are you?"

"No." He pushed his plate away. "I'm not married now, nor have I ever been married."

She lifted her chin and folded her arms across her chest. "Are you romantically or sexually involved with someone else? Considering the times, I think I deserve to know."

He stood and crossed to her. He looked her directly in the eye. "No. And I haven't been involved with anyone—romantically or sexually—for a long time."

She opened her mouth to ask another question, then shut it and turned to face the sink. For long moments he stared at her stiff back and shoulders, then he gently turned her to him. "I can't talk about this, Annabelle. Not yet."

"No problem."

But it was a problem. For her. And him. He felt it between them like a wall. And he felt like a total heel. "The errand will take an hour. Two, tops. We'll talk when I get back." He cupped her face, forcing her to meet his gaze. "Trust me on this, okay?"

She smiled slowly. It warmed him more than it should have. "Okay."

The doctor's office was located across from the courthouse on Main Street in downtown Ames. Downtown Ames was a collection of shops and offices located around a grassy square. Magnolias dotted the square, although not one of them could compete with Ashland's Sweethearts' Magnolia.

Dr. Garner was younger than Rush had thought he would be. Tall and thin, with thick dark hair and wearing wire-rimmed spectacles, he was the picture of a Southern gentleman.

Rush held his hand out. "Dr. Garner, thank you for seeing me. I know how busy you must be."

The young doctor smiled and motioned Rush to sit down. "Your call intrigued me, Mr. Cousins. I went ahead and did a little digging."

Rush took the seat across from the doctor's. "And?"

"There were no Cousins in the county, or if they were, they never required any medical treatment." Pete Garner looked at him over steepled fingers. "You're sure you're from around here?"

Rush made a sound of frustration and leaned forward in his seat. "No, I'm not sure. I believe I am. I believe, strongly, that I spent time at Ashland Plantation as a young boy. But I can't be sure."

"And the name Cousins? That's your birth name?"

"That's the name the woman who brought me to the orphanage told the nuns." Rush stood and crossed to the small window that faced the square. A group of young boys were playing touch football. "Which, of course, could or could not be true."

"I went through my father's files and checked the birth record of every boy born the years you believe you were." The doctor inclined his head. "These files represent the infants I can't personally account for. All the others I either know or have heard of the family. You're welcome to go through them. I'm sorry, but I can't let you remove them from the office."

Rush turned back to the doctor. In his eyes Rush saw genuine sympathy. "Thanks."

"Well, I have a lot of paperwork to catch up on, so I'll leave you to it." Pete Garner stood and crossed to the door. There, he stopped and rubbed his chin thoughtfully. "You know, sometimes girls got into trouble... and the family kept it secret. They usually used a midwife or another relative to deliver the baby, then shipped it off. Times were different. My father would have known about it, even if he wasn't the attending physician. He may be able to help you."

"Is there any way I could contact him?"

"He's coming to town for my daughter's fourth birthday."

"When?"

"Two weeks." Pete Garner shook his head. "He's getting up there, though. His memory's not as good as it used to be."

"Thanks." Rush smiled. "I really do appreciate your going out of your way like this."

"I can empathize. At least a little." Pete Garner returned his smile. "My wife's adopted. It's always bugged her, not knowing who she is." He paused. "I wish you luck."

Chapter Nine

Where was Rush?

Anna carried a glass of iced tea onto the gallery. Too restless to sit and rock, Anna set down the glass and crossed to the edge of the gallery. She scanned the River Road as far as she could see, then made a sound of disappointment.

Rush had promised he would be gone for only an hour or two. It had already been over three. She tipped her face to the cloudless sky. The sun, already losing the potency of afternoon, had begun its descent into evening, while shadows stretched their long fingers over Ashland's grounds.

She turned her gaze once more to the road. Her day had been an exercise in strength of will. It had taken all of hers to keep her mind on the walls she was sanding, and to maintain an air of normalcy despite the fear clawing at the pit of her stomach. Fear that he regretted having made love with her, fear that she might never see him again.

And the certainty that something wasn't right.

Anna returned her gaze to the road. Where had he gone? she wondered for about the millionth time. What was he keeping from her?

Anna leaned against the column, its plaster cool despite the heat of the day. Rush had offered her nothing; yet she wanted everything from him.

His secrets. Commitment. Love.

She should take what he offered and be grateful for it. He'd already given her more than she'd believed she would ever have—freedom from her past, freedom from the fear of failure, a self-confidence she'd never felt before. It should be enough.

It wasn't. Not by a long shot.

Anna plucked a leaf from a wild vine that had crept up one of the columns. She held it to her nose. He'd promised he would be careful with her, that he wouldn't hurt her. He'd asked her to trust him. It scared her silly, but she would.

Besides, what other choice did she have? She loved him.

Travis's Mercedes sedan pulled into the drive, and Anna watched the car wind down the drive until it disappeared around the side of the house. She sighed. She wasn't up for a visit from Travis today. Because of Rush. And because she hadn't been able to put what Lowell had told her out of her head. That Travis would even consider buying half of Ashland from her brother hurt like hell.

Moments later, Travis rounded the house, lifting his hand in greeting. She returned his wave, but couldn't bring herself to smile.

"Anna." Travis stepped onto the gallery and crossed to her. "I'm glad I caught you taking a break."

"Hello, Travis." She heard the hesitation in her own voice—the coolness—and cursed it. She'd never felt any way but open and safe with Travis before. Now she felt guarded. Like she couldn't completely trust him anymore. All because of Lowell's selfishness and irresponsibility. She would never forgive her brother if he'd put a permanent wedge between her and Travis.

Travis bent and kissed her cheek. When he pulled away, he gazed at her for a long moment, his expression thoughtful. "You look radiant," he murmured, straightening.

Radiant? Anna stared at him in surprise. Had her feelings for Rush manifested themselves in her appearance? Did Travis know, just by looking at her, that she and Rush had become lovers? At the thought, her cheeks heated.

"You know, Anna," he continued, his voice deepening, "I've always thought you were beautiful."

He'd surprised her again. He'd never spoken to her this way before. Never looked at her in any way but in friendship. She should be flattered, pleased; but it made her uncomfortable instead.

She laced her fingers. "Well...I... Thank you, Travis."

"I should have told you before, but..." He shook his head and turned away from her. Crossing to one of the massive columns, he gazed out at Ashland's grounds.

Anna stared at his stiff back, sensing his discomfort. She feared she understood it, but prayed she was wrong. "Why did you come out here today, Travis? What's on your mind?"

"You are, Anna. And Ashland."

Her heart began to thump uncomfortably against the wall of her chest, and she clasped her hands in front of her. "I'll help you out," she said. "Lowell told me about the reason for your visit the other day. He told me about the offer he made you."

"I thought so. I could tell by your...tone." He turned and met her eyes. "We know each other too well to hide anything."

She shifted her gaze, thinking again of Rush, of their lovemaking. That was something she had no intention of showing. Or sharing.

"I'm sorry about that day. I knew what you must have been thinking, how you must have felt. I hated putting you in that position. I resented Lowell for making me choose, even if only for those minutes."

She inched her chin up, tears pricking at the backs of her eyes. "It hurt, Trav. It hurt to think you would consider buying half of Ashland. You know what it means to me."

"Yes, I know." He turned away from her again to stare out at the magnolia canopy. "I love Ashland, too. I always have." He looked over his shoulder at her once more. "You know that, don't you?"

Something in his expression tugged at her, and she nodded. "Yes, I know."

A frustrated smile twisted his mouth. "I always wanted to be a part of this place. To belong here. I used to dream of it."

And now he had a chance to make his dreams come true. He'd decided to take Lowell up on his offer.

How could he do this to her?

"What are you trying to tell me, Trav?"

"I'm not trying to tell you anything. I'm..." He swore softly and looked away. "Remember how the gardens used to be? Remember in the spring? How full and fragrant?" He laughed softly. "The bumblebees were as big as my thumb."

She laughed, too. "Remember the one that chased us clear into the house? We didn't go near the garden for a week."

Travis turned and crossed to where she stood. Stopping before her, he gathered her hands in his. "The gardens could be that way again, Anna. And the house could be magnificent. We could restore Ashland to her former glory. It could be everything it once was."

"You told Lowell yes," she whispered, unable to hide the hurt, the betrayal, she felt. Her eyes swam with tears. "How could you? You're my friend."

He squeezed her fingers. "I told him no."

"But... you said we—"

"Marry me, Anna."

For long moments, she stared at him, too shocked to speak. Then she shook her head. "You didn't just ask me to..."

"But I did." He brought her hands to his mouth. "Say yes, Anna. Say you'll marry me."

"Travis, I... You've... surprised me. I didn't expect...this." She slipped her hands from his and turned away from him, working to gather her thoughts. "We've known each other a long time, but we've never... It's never been romantic between us."

"We could remedy that." He caught her elbow and turned her back to him. "This makes sense, Anna. We grew up together. We know and understand each other. We like each other. And we both love Ashland."

"Oh, Travis..." She shook her head. "I—"

"Wait." He touched his index finger to her mouth. "Before you say anything, consider this. We're both alone. Forty and alone isn't what I want. Is it what you want? I don't think so. I love children and so do you. We love Ashland. We could be happy. I know we could."

A month ago, a week ago even, she would have considered his offer. She might even have said yes. But a month ago she hadn't been in love with another man. A month ago she hadn't realized how wonderful romance and passion could be. How necessary.

"Oh, Travis." She stroked his cheek lightly, hating to hurt him, knowing that she had no choice. "I do love you... as a friend. And I'm flattered by your offer, but—"

He made a sound of frustration. Of disappointment. "But no."

"No. I can't. I..." Her words trailed off as Rush drove up, tooting the horn. She saw that the back of the pickup was loaded with wood.

Travis followed her gaze. "I see."

She looked back at her old friend. Her eyes filled at the bitterness in his expression, the hurt. "Am I so transparent?"

"Yes."

She squeezed his hand. "I'm sorry, Travis."

"Don't be." He smiled sadly, all traces of bitterness gone. "And don't rule this out, not just yet." When she opened her mouth to argue, he laid a finger against her lips. "Think it over, Anna. Take some time. Promise me you'll at least give it some thought?"

She nodded and he drew her against his chest. "People come and go," he murmured, pressing his lips to her hair. "But I'll be here, Annabelle. I'll always be here."

Tears pricked her eyes again, but this time because she understood what he was saying to her. Rush was a drifter. He wouldn't stay. Travis was telling her that he would wait, that he would still want her when Rush was gone.

But she would never want anyone but Rush.

Anna walked Travis to his car. Rush was there, unloading the lumber from the back. The two men glared at each other, neither speaking.

Travis climbed into his car, started it, then looked up at her. "Think about what you really want. Take some time. I'll call you."

Anna watched him drive off, her chest tight with tears. She'd hurt the only man who had ever stood by her and loved her no matter what, the only man who had never let her down.

It wasn't her fault. She couldn't marry a man she didn't love, especially when she was so desperately in love with another. It wouldn't be fair to her; it wouldn't be fair to Travis.

But she couldn't deny the ache of regret building inside her. The feeling that somehow, she could have prevented this from happening.

Just as she couldn't deny the knot of anger.

She swung around and faced Rush, all the frustration and worry of the day, the second-guessing and insecurity, boiling to the surface, demanding release.

Anna sensed a responding anger in him, A frustration and tightly leashed violence. He, too, was spoiling for a fight.

Rush narrowed his eyes. "That looked mighty cozy, Annabelle. Maybe I should have stayed away longer."

The blood rushed to her head. "Maybe you should have. Maybe all afternoon wasn't enough."

She tried to push by him; he stopped her. His hand on her arm felt like a vise. "What did Gentry want?"

"Why do you want to know?" she demanded, so angry she shook. "What business is it of yours?"

"Don't play games, Anna. They're not your style."

She shook her arm free of his grasp. "But they are yours, aren't they?"

"What's that supposed to mean?"

"I'll be gone an hour," she mimicked. "Two, tops? It's been four. At least."

"I got tied up."

"And I'm not supposed to ask why. Right? I'm not supposed to be angry that you didn't call. I'm not supposed to worry. That would be a lie. And that's a game I don't play."

She dragged a trembling hand through her hair, searching for a modicum of control. She found it. Barely. "You demanded honesty and trust from me. I expect the same from you. If you feel you can give me that, you'll know where to find me."

She turned and started for the house; he followed her. When he caught up, he swung her around to face him. "What did Travis want?"

"He asked me to marry him. Satisfied?"

Rush tightened his fingers; a muscle jumped in his clenched jaw. "And what was your answer, Annabelle? Did you say yes?"

At his question, Anna caught her breath. The bit of control she'd managed to find went careening out of her reach. "How could you even ask that?" She jerked her arm free of his grasp. "How could you even think I wo—"

"Did you?"

"No." She pushed her hair away from her face with trembling fingers. "I told him no."

"Big mistake, Anna." He took a step toward her, eyes glittering, jaw tight. "He has money. Position. He could help you rebuild Ashland."

Pain curled through her, twisting, tightening. She cocked her chin. "You don't know me very well if you think I would sleep with one man, then turn around and agree to marry another."

He cupped her face in his palms. "Don't get too attached, Annabelle. I won't be staying. I can't."

"I see." Tears built behind her eyes and she fought against them, fought against him seeing how much his words hurt her.

"I don't think you do." He moved his fingers to her hair. She sensed a desperation in the way he held on to her. "It's not you, Anna. It's me." He searched her gaze. "I want you to know that. I want you to believe it."

But if he loved her, he would stay.

She shook her head. "Drifters don't make commitments, do they? This isn't news, you know."

He searched her expression. "Isn't it?"

She hurt so badly she wanted to curl into a ball under the covers and never come out. Instead she stiffened her spine. "Maybe you're right. Maybe I should marry Travis. But exactly how would this work? Would I sleep with one of you or both of you?"

Rush dropped his hands to her shoulders. "Stop it, Anna."

"In fact, now that you've gotten me through this freezing thing—"

"Anna, I'm warning you." He jerked her against his chest, the expression in his eyes murderous.

"—why don't I just try making it with everybody? If it's great with one partner, it must be grand with a doz—"

Rush's mouth crashed down on hers, capturing her words. The force of his kiss bent her backward, and she clung to him, curling her fingers into the fabric of his shirt.

When he released her, she took a step back from him, her legs trembling so badly she feared she might stumble. "I'm not the kind of woman who would make commitments, even if only physical, to more than one man. Don't offend me like that again."

She shook her head. "You can't have it both ways, Rush. You can't dismiss me on the one hand and act like the jealous lover on the other. Either you care or you don't. This may not be permanent, but it's either exclusive or it's nothing. Now excuse me, I'm going in."

Ashland had never been so quiet. It had never seemed so empty. Anna laid her novel on the floor next to her and turned her gaze to the parlor windows and the black night beyond. How had Rush changed her life so quickly? One short month ago, she would have found the quiet peaceful. Relaxing.

Now it just felt . . . lonely.

Had she changed his life at all? she wondered, leaning her head against the back of the settee. A lump formed in her throat. Probably not. He was much more important to her than she'd ever been to him.

She drew in a deep breath, even though it hurt. Since their fight that afternoon, she'd asked herself those same questions dozens of times. She'd also asked herself if she'd made the right decision.

And every time, she'd answered herself yes. No matter how badly she hurt or how much she missed him, she couldn't compromise her integrity. She had to have honesty from him. She had to have trust. Even when it hurt like the devil.

Beside her, Blue whined and thumped his tail against the oak flooring. She smiled at him and scratched his chest. "You miss him, too, don't you, boy?"

The big dog rolled his eyes and laid his head back, whining again. She smoothed her hand over his massive rib cage, then tickled his underbelly. "So, Baby Blue, what are we going to do with our time?"

As if in answer to her question, a knock sounded at the door, echoing through the empty house. Anna sucked in a quick breath, hope surging through her. Could it be Rush? Her heart told her it was, told her he'd made a decision about their relationship. The one she hoped he'd made.

But her head told her not to get her hopes up, not to set herself up for an even bigger hurt.

Blue jumped up and raced for the door. When he reached it he began pawing at it and whimpering.

She had her answer. Blue was as crazy about Rush as she was.

Standing, she wiped her damp palms on the seat of her jeans and told herself to get a grip. If he'd made a decision, there was nothing she could do about it now.

Drawing in a deep breath, she crossed to the door and swung it open.

Rush stood on the other side of the door, a duffel bag slung over his shoulder, his expression tense. Anna eyed the bag, biting her lip to keep from crying out.

He'd made his decision, all right. He'd decided to leave.

"May I come in?"

She stared at him for a moment, then swung the door open and stepped aside so he could enter. Without speaking, she led him to the front parlor.

Rush set his duffel bag carefully on the settee, then met her eyes. "I'm not the best at apologies, but I'll give it a try. I behaved like a bastard this afternoon. I'm sorry."

Tears stung her eyes, and she nodded. "Apology accepted."

Turning, he crossed to a window and stared out at the darkness. "And you were right," he continued after a moment, "I demanded honesty from you, but refused you the same courtesy."

He looked over his shoulder at her. "I don't share myself easily. When you open yourself up, you invite a knife. It's a matter of survival, Annabelle."

Anna lifted her chin, fighting tears. "But I trusted you, Rush. *I* opened myself up. In a way I never had before."

He looked away again. "I know. That meant a lot to me."

It had meant a lot to him, all right, she thought bitterly, eyeing the duffel bag once more. That's why he was getting the hell out of Dodge in such a hurry.

Rush began to pace. He moved to the bookcase, from there to the fireplace, and then to another of her mother's drawings. This one depicted her and Lowell picnicking under the magnolias.

Rush stared at it for long moments, then faced her once more. "I told you about being dumped at St. Catherine's Orphanage when I was five. What I didn't tell you was, the woman who brought me there wasn't my mother. At least the nuns felt certain she wasn't. She was dirty and practically illiterate. She stank of sweat and old booze.''

Rush's expression tightened, and he flexed his fingers as if controlling a great emotion. ''And, they tell me,'' he went on, ''that I was frightened of her. I didn't cry when she left me, only clung, terrified, to one of the Sisters. They speculated that she'd either found me on the street or...that one of my parents had paid her to deliver me to St Catherine's. To avoid questions or paperwork. Or even the possibility of being turned away. St. Catherine's contacted the police and Children's Services, but nothing ever came of it.''

Tears formed a lump in Anna's throat. How awful for him. How painful. ''So...you don't know anything about your family or birth?''

''Not even the day or year.'' His lips twisted. ''The only clue to my lineage was my Southern accent.''

''But you were five. Surely you had some—''

''Memory?'' He shook his head. ''None. But I suffered from terrible nightmares. Night after night my screams awakened everyone.''

Anna clasped her hands in front of her, battling tears. Tears for a terrified little boy. A little boy with no memory and no one to love him. ''Oh, Rush. I'm so sorry.''

He went on as if she hadn't spoken. ''To this day, I don't remember the first five years of my life. It's a giant, dark void. Sometimes the memories visit in my dreams, but they're shadows only. Impressions.''

''Last night, when I awoke and you were gone—''

''Yes.'' He moved restlessly around the room, touching this and that, less interested, Anna thought, in the things than in the movement. "I wasn't a charming child, not the type who attracted parents. I was withdrawn and sullen, haunted by nightmares. I went through foster families fast."

He smiled, but the curving of his lips was devoid of humor. "I found that people take children in for a lot of different reasons. To be playmates for their own children or little helpers for them. Some do it for the additional income. Never, in my experience, because they want to love and help a child grow."

Anna heard the hurt in his voice, although he would have denied it was there. She heard the longing. She imagined him as a boy, longing to be loved and accepted, being disappointed again and again.

She wanted to touch him, to try to comfort him. She took a step toward him, hand out. "Rush, I'm..."

He shook his head. "Don't, Anna. I need to finish. After you know everything, if you still want..." He left the thought unsaid, and returned to the window and the blackness beyond. "By the time I was ten, I'd become a brawler. A troublemaker. I instigated a lot of fights. Luckily I was big for my age. I didn't get hurt badly too many times. My aggression was a form of self-defense, I realize now. A survival technique. When you don't have an adult to look out for your interests, you're an easy mark. For other children. Adults. The bad guys."

She couldn't imagine the Rush she knew as a street fighter or bully. She thought of the way he'd held and stroked her, the way he'd helped her through her fear. Where had he learned about tenderness? About empathy? Who had taught him to be gentle?

"Finally, I took off. I'd had it with the system. It was a joke. And I felt I was old enough to take care of myself."

"How old were you?" she asked softly, unsure she wanted to know the answer.

"Fifteen. Almost."

Almost? My God, he'd been hardly more than a baby. She brought a hand to her mouth. "But where . . . did you live? What did you do to—"

"Survive?" He laughed without humor. "Whatever I had to. I took some odd jobs. Stole to eat, if I had to. Or ate garbage. You'd be surprised what some people throw out. I was one of the lucky ones. I wasn't on the streets that long. A guy caught me picking his pocket. Instead of calling the police, he gave me a job. He was a carpenter. He owned his own business."

"And you got your start."

"Yeah." Rush's face softened. "Jack Madigan was the only truly kind man I had ever met. His only son had been killed in a car wreck. His wife had run off with another guy. I guess we needed each other. He took me under his wing."

"What happened to him?"

"I left him behind." Rush met her eyes. "I leave everyone behind, Anna."

Tears swamped her eyes, and she fought them back. She'd been right from the outset—he'd come to say goodbye. But she'd hoped she was wrong; had hoped he'd decided he needed her.

"I learned a lot about kindness from him. I learned about trust. I learned about the way people were supposed to live."

She clasped her hands together. She wanted this over with. If he was going to end it, she wanted him to do it now. Cleanly. Swiftly. And then leave her alone to mourn. "Why are you telling me this, Rush? Why don't you just—"

"Because you deserve to know," he interrupted, closing the distance between them. "Because I should have told you from the first."

He cupped her face in his palms, and gazed at her with an intensity that made her knees weak. And had her almost believing that he cared for her. "What are you trying to tell me?" she asked softly.

"Today I went to see Dr. Garner. That's where I was this afternoon. He'd agreed to talk to me, and I couldn't pass on the opportunity."

"Dr. Garner?" She drew her eyebrows together. "Are you sick?"

He shook his head and went to the duffel bag. He took out an object wrapped in towels and brought it to her. "This is for you, Anna."

She looked in confusion from him to the object, then took it. Carefully, she peeled away the towels. Her heart stopped, then started again at a manic pace.

"My music box," she whispered, stunned. "My beautiful music box." She lifted her eyes to his. "But where did you... How did you..."

At his expression, her hands began to shake. "Rush? How long have you... had this?"

"It brought me here."

"I don't understand."

"I bought the box in Boston. The dealer knew where it was from. She must have bought it from Lowell."

"But I... still don't understand why you... came here. Why did it bring you to Ashland?"

He drew a deep breath, and for the first time tonight, she saw excitement in his eyes. When he spoke, she heard it in his voice. "Anna, I put my hands on the music box and I remembered. I knew its tune before it began to play. You can't imagine what it felt like to touch a piece of my past. To finally…get a glimmer of what I'd lost. It was incredible, like a brilliant light penetrating darkness."

He took the music box from her, curving his hands around it. "I didn't know when I'd touched it before, I only knew that I had. For the first time in my life the shadows were almost within my grasp."

Anna went to the settee and sank onto it. "So…you came to Ashland looking for…" She lifted her gaze to his. "What, Rush? What did you hope to find here?"

"My past," he said simply. "I came to find out who I am."

"I see."

"And the house I'm staying in, I recognized it, too." He began pacing again, this time like a caged animal. "But nothing else. Not yet. It feels right being here— the heat, the smells—but nothing like what I felt with the box."

Anna thought of his questions, his seemingly casual curiosity about her family, about the plantation. She remembered the night he'd looked at the drawing of her and the music box, remembered telling him about it, and a sob rose in her throat. "You lied to me."

He stopped pacing and met her eyes. His were filled with regret. "I kept the truth from you. There's a difference."

"A damn slim one." She clasped her hands in her lap. "You're not a drifter, are you?"

"I own my own building-and-restoration firm. In Boston."

"I see." She lowered her eyes to her hands and drew in a shaky breath. "I thought the way you just showed up at Ashland, out of the blue, was some sort of small miracle. I couldn't believe my luck."

"It was lucky. For both of us." He crossed to her and she lifted her gaze to his. "It was almost as if…as if somebody was watching out for us, as if somebody put us together to—"

"Oh, please."

She tried to stand; he caught her hands. "Think about it. Think about how desperate you were to find skilled help to repair Ashland. And me, I'd given up on finding my past. I'd told myself I didn't care."

She searched his gaze, her heart breaking. Finding his past. That's all this had been for him, all they had been to him. But it had been so much more for her than having help to repair Ashland.

"I need your help, Anna. To find my connection to this place, to find out who I am."

She made a sound filled with self-derision. All along, she'd wondered what he'd wanted with her. Annabelle Ames, the almost-forty, plain and prim spinster. She'd allowed herself to start believing in him, in herself, in miracles.

What a naive fool she'd been. What an idiot.

She lifted her chin. "Was that what…last night was all about? Helping you?" She could hardly form the words, it hurt so badly. They came out small and choked. "Is that why you…why we…"

"God, no." He squatted down in front of her and gathered her hands in his. "Last night had nothing to do with anything but you and me and this thing we feel between us.''

She jerked her hands from his and stood, a sob rising and catching in her throat. ''You expect me to believe that? After the way you lied? After the way you used me? All along, the only thing you cared about was finding out your past.''

''That's not true.''

''Then why didn't you tell me right away? Why weren't you up front with me about this?''

He swore. ''I should have been. And if I had to do it over again, I would be.''

She crossed to the window. ''Great.''

''I was afraid you'd turn me away,'' he said quietly. ''I couldn't take that chance.''

''I trusted you,'' she said, her voice shaking uncontrollably. ''You asked me to trust you. You promised you wouldn't hurt me. You *have* hurt me. You lied to me. You deceived me.''

''I didn't mean to, Anna.'' He took a step toward her, hand out. ''I never wanted to hurt you. Just as I didn't mean to get personally involved with you. This thing between us just snowballed, and before I knew it, we were—''

''It doesn't snow in Mississippi, Rush.'' She curved her arms around herself. ''I want you to leave.''

''Anna…'' He took a step toward her, hand out. ''If you'd just put aside your hurt for a moment and think about—''

''I asked you to leave,'' she said as haughtily as she could. ''I won't ask you again.''

Rush stopped, his expression hardening. ''Nobody has to ask me to leave more than once.'' He snatched his empty duffel from the settee. "Have a nice night, princess."

And then he was gone.

As the slam of the door resounded through Ashland, Anna sank onto the floor beside Blue and cried.

Chapter Ten

Sleep eluded Anna. She tossed and turned; she lay awake for hours, staring at the ceiling, unable to think of anything but Rush's betrayal.

When he'd walked out he'd acted like he was angry. What had he had to be angry about? He'd lied to her; he'd used her.

He'd let her down. Just as every man she'd ever known, in one way or another, had let her down.

She groaned and pulled the pillow over her face. How had she been such a fool? How could she have believed he was interested in her? Attracted to her?

She tossed the pillow aside and sat up. Ashland. It always came back to Ashland. Her father and brother. Her fiancé. Travis. Now Rush. In one way or another, every relationship she'd ever had with a man had been colored—or tainted—by Ashland.

She was some sort of package deal, she thought, feeling for the first time in her life a modicum of the bitterness Lowell felt, a modicum of the dislike for Ashland that Lowell had.

She ran her fingers along the embroidered edge of the rumpled top sheet. Without Ashland, would her life be different? Would it be better? The way Lowell was always telling her. Would she be loved?

From the floor beside the bed, Blue growled. Anna sat up straighter, pulling the sheet to her breasts, listening. She heard nothing but emptiness. She opened her mouth to reassure Blue when she heard the creak of the stairs.

Someone was in the house.

Blue got to his feet, growling again, low in his throat. Anna caught her breath. Reaching out, she laid a hand on the dog, to reassure herself and to keep him by her side. The hair on his back stood up and beneath her hand, his body tensed, as if readying for attack.

She heard footfalls in the hall. Heart pounding, she slipped her hand under the pillow, curving her fingers around the cold steel of her gun. She'd never had to use it before. She'd never been forced to face the reality of aiming it at someone with the intent of firing.

The thought turned her stomach.

Gripping the weapon with both hands, she released the safety and aimed at the door. "Who's there?" she called out, trying to sound confident but sounding terrified instead.

Her door swung open; her heart leapt to her throat. "Anna . . . it's me. Lowell."

Lowell? Her breath shuddered past her lips and she lowered the gun. She realized she was sweating.

"Don't ever do that to me again!" she snapped. Dropping the gun onto the bed as if it were red-hot, she brought her shaking hands to her face. "I could have shot you!"

"It's not too late, sis."

"Very funny." She reached for the light. "Haven't you ever heard of the telephone? And what are you doing out here so late? It's the middle of the..."

Anna gasped as light flooded the room. Her brother had been in a fight. Half his face was swollen, the skin purpling; his blond hair was matted with something ominously dark on one side. His clothes were ripped and muddy.

"My God, Lowell!" She jumped out of bed and raced to his side. "What happened?"

He managed a weak smile. "I crossed the wrong guys."

She put her arm around him and helped him to the bed. He groaned as he sank onto the mattress, and she arranged the pillows so he could sit up. He leaned against them, closing his eyes and making a sound of exhaustion and pain as he did.

Anna gazed at him, a lump in her throat. His skin looked pasty, even against the bright white of the sheets. Except where it was turning purple, except for the deep, hollow shadows under his eyes. He looked like he'd lost ten pounds since she'd seen him last.

Dear God, what was happening to him?

"I'll be back," she whispered, shocked that she could even find her voice. "I'll get an ice pack and something to clean you up."

Minutes later, she tiptoed back into her bedroom, expecting him to be asleep. Instead, he sat in the bed, his eyes wide. In them she saw something wild, something out of control.

"I brought you a nice cup of chamomile tea." She forced a smile. "Just what the doctor ordered."

Lowell made a face. "I believe the doctor ordered something a bit stronger."

She sat the tray on the nightstand, then positioned herself on the edge of the bed beside him. "Don't you think you've had enough of that?" She handed him the ice pack.

His lips twisted. "My Florence Nightingale. What would I do without you?"

"If you don't like it here, go check into the nearest E.R." She dipped a washcloth in the bowl of warm water she'd brought up, soaking it. Carefully, she began to clean the wound on his head, wiping away the dried blood.

"Who did this to you?" she asked, working to control the tremor in her voice.

"The bad guys."

She frowned. "Funny."

"You never did like my sense of humor." He winced as she dabbed at the cut. "Hey, that hurts."

"I don't see anything funny about this." He didn't reply, so she pressed. "What's going on Lowell?"

"I already told you, I made enemies of the wrong guys."

She dropped the cloth in the bowl, then gently probed the gash with her fingers. "I think you're okay without stitches. But you might want to have Dr. Garner take a look at it anyway."

"That stiff? Forget it."

She shook her head and took out the antiseptic. "This is going to sting."

She applied the medicine, and he howled. "Take it easy with that stuff, will you?"

She rolled her eyes and dabbed at it again. "Have you called the police?"

"These are not the kind of people you report to the police." He fumbled in his pocket for his cigarettes, swearing when he found the pack was empty.

"No police, Lowell?"

He looked away. "No."

"What kind of trouble *have* you gotten yourself into?" she asked, hearing the fear in her own voice. "What kind of people are these?"

"I've run up some debt," he said after a moment. "They want their money."

"What kind of debt?" He just looked at her, and she swore.

"Dammit, Lowell! Daddy blew everything on gambling and now you—"

"I'm nothing like him," Lowell snapped, clenching his hands into fists. "Don't ever mention us in the same breath like that again."

"Oh, excuse me." She arched her eyebrows. "Daddy lost everything on gambling and drinking. Now you're doing the same. But you're nothing like him? For Pete's sake, Lowell. Didn't you learn anything by his example?"

"This was different."

"Right."

She made a sound of disgust and started to stand. He caught her hand and pulled her back to the bed. "This was a one-shot deal. A sure thing."

"If it was such a sure thing, why are you in trouble?"

His face fell. "I don't know. I was so certain that this time..." He curled his fingers around hers. "I need your help, Anna. You've got to help me."

Rush had uttered those same words to her just a few short hours ago. Pain speared through her. Every man in her life had always wanted something from her. But would anyone ever just want her? For herself? Would anyone ever love her—unreservedly and without strings?

She slipped her hand from her brother's and stood. Crossing to the window, she inched aside the drape and stared out at the night. Tonight the sky was without stars, the moon obscured by clouds.

She thought of another night, one bathed in golden moonlight. The night she and Rush had made love. Tears clogged her throat. Had it only been the night before? It felt as if years had passed since then.

"You've got to help me, sis."

She wheeled around, shaking with anger and frustration. "Do I, Lowell? Do I 'have' to?"

"They're going to break my legs."

"Oh, please. Give me a little more credit than that."

"It's true." He pulled himself a little farther up in the bed. "They said—"

"How much, Lowell?"

"Fifteen thousand."

She lifted her eyebrows. "Fifteen thousand?" she repeated. "A few weeks ago, Travis told me you needed ten."

He shifted his gaze. "Interest."

She stared at him, shocked, repulsed. She took a step toward him, her fingers clenched. "Do you have any idea how much money that is? Do you have any idea how long and how hard I have to work to make that much?''

She shook her head, incredulous. "You don't, do you? You've never worked for anything. You have no concept of..." She shook her head again. "We're not the rich Ameses anymore. It's over, Lowell. It has been for a long time."

Her brother dragged a shaking hand through his hair, wincing at the movement. "You don't understand. I have nowhere else to turn."

The adrenaline of anger surged through her. "And just how do you expect me to help you? I don't have—''

"You could marry Travis," he said quickly. "I know he wants you. He would take care of us. He—''

"Marry Travis?" she repeated, furious, insulted. "So, you would basically...pimp me to pay off your gambling debts!''

"It wouldn't be like that! Dammit, Anna, I didn't mean that!'' He climbed out of bed and crossed to where she stood. She could tell it took great effort to do so. "He's a good guy. He loves us, loves Ash—''

"I don't love him, Lowell. The answer is no."

He caught her hands. "There's another way."

She knew what was coming and shook her head. "We've been through this before. I won't sell Ashland."

"Why not? It makes sense. It would be good for both of us. Several interested parties answered my ads, but they all wanted the whole thing. One called it an architectural plum.'' He squeezed her fingers, excited. "Just think how much we could get for it.''

She made a sound of pain and disbelief. "You're so selfish, Lowell. So self-consumed. Sell our ancestral home to pay your gambling debts? You *are* like Daddy."

He caught her arm, gripping so tightly she winced. "You're the one who's like him. Believing all that bull he dished out, believing all those stupid, overblown stories of his."

"Same old song, Lowell. Everybody has a problem but you." She shook off his hand. "I'm not the one who's in trouble. I'm not the one who's sick."

She walked to the bed and snatched up one of the pillows and a blanket. "You're not a child. You have to take care of yourself. You have to grow up. I'm not going to take care of you anymore."

"Anna—"

"No." She looked him in the eye. "Ashland isn't Daddy, Lowell. Selling it isn't going to kill your memory of him. It's not going to change how you feel about yourself."

"I feel fine." He gripped the window frame for support, making his words even more laughable. "Great, in fact. I just need a good night's sleep and someone who cares enough about me to lend me the money I need."

She hugged the pillow and blanket to her chest, fighting tears. "You hated Daddy, and you had a right to. He treated you . . . terribly. But you've done everything in your power to become just like him. It doesn't make any sense. And you're miserable."

"I haven't become like him."

She started for the door, stopping and looking over her shoulder at him when she reached it. "Grow up, baby brother. It's time."

"You're not going to help me." He shook his head as if he couldn't comprehend it. "They're going to hurt me. Don't you understand? Don't you care?"

She gazed at him, pity warring with love. "I do understand. And I do care about you."

"Then help me." His voice deepened. "I'm begging you, Anna."

The despair on his face tore at her and for a moment, she thought of relenting. Of giving in to him. Only thirty minutes ago she'd been wondering what her life would be like without the burden—and lure—of Ashland.

Anna looked into his eyes and firmed her resolve. She'd gotten him out of scrapes too many times. Everyone had. Their mama had always made excuses for him. So had she. And Macy. It was time Lowell learned to stand on his own two feet. It was time he learned that some behavior there was no excuse for.

"Take my bed, I'll sleep on the settee."

"Annabelle, please..."

Anna shook her head. "Prove you're not like Daddy," she murmured. "You say you're not, Lowell. Prove it."

Turning, she left him alone.

When Anna awakened the next morning, Lowell was gone. He hadn't left a note; it didn't look as if he'd eaten anything. In truth, she wasn't even sure he'd stayed the night.

Anna stared at her rumpled bed, frowning. What was her brother going to do with his life? She'd asked him to prove he wasn't like their father, but she feared he didn't have the strength of will, the personal fortitude, to pull himself back from whatever precipice he stood at the edge of.

She would help him; she wanted to help him. But first he had to want to help himself.

She quickly stripped the bed and carried the bundle of sheets down to the laundry room. She dumped them in the basket, then went to the kitchen to make her breakfast. Sunlight tumbled through the windows. She crossed to one and gazed out at the new day. Summer was in full bloom, a riot of brilliant colors and lush scents.

Anna touched the warm glass and smiled. She didn't feel sad this morning. She didn't feel hopeless or tired. And she wasn't certain why.

Maybe it was because she hadn't allowed Lowell to hurt her the night before. Maybe it was because, for the first time, she'd dealt with him as an adult.

But what of Rush? Her smile faded. The hurt had dulled, becoming a hollow ache. She didn't want to think about him. She wouldn't, not now.

Acting on a whim, she packed herself a muffin and a container of juice and walked down the magnolia grove to the river. She sat on the soft levee grass and ate her breakfast, gazing out at the sleepy Mississippi.

Anna sighed. She'd spent many of her childhood mornings this way, sometimes alone, but usually with her mother. They'd laughed and talked and collected wildflowers. And she'd known, without a shadow of a doubt, that she was loved.

She shifted her gaze from the river to Ashland. Her home. Home to dozens of Ameses before her. Her safety net, the thing that kept her grounded.

She belonged here.

Tell me what it feels like to belong.

Rush's words from a conversation weeks ago came barreling back into her head and tears pricked at her eyes. The thing she cherished most in the world, Rush had never known.

What must that feel like? she wondered, digging her fingers into the soft mat of grass. Her sense of belonging was so deeply ingrained in who she was, she couldn't imagine not having it.

Just as she couldn't imagine not knowing who she was.

Another thing that Rush had never had.

I want to know who I am. There's a difference.

She remembered the expression in his eyes when he'd said those words, remembered the grim line of his jaw. It had tugged at her heartstrings then, it tore at them now.

She plucked a blade of grass and trailed it thoughtfully across her bottom lip. What had happened to Rush in those five missing years of his life? she wondered. Who were his parents? And how could they have discarded him?

Anna thought of the music box, of his happening upon it in some shop. It was a one-of-a-kind piece. How had he recognized it? *Could* his past somehow be connected to Ashland? To her?

She tried to put herself in his place. Tried to imagine his shock, his wonder, when he put his hands on the box and almost remembered. He'd described it as a brilliant light penetrating darkness.

Her heart began to pound. How excited he must have been. How stunned. It must have been like a miracle for him.

And so he had come to Ashland, searching for answers.

And had changed her life.

Anna sucked in a shaky breath, collected the remains of her breakfast and stood. Rush wasn't like Lowell. He wasn't like any man she'd ever known. He was kind. And gentle.

But most of all, he was strong. She started down the levee, going toward the overseer's house. Rush had overcome impossible odds and made something out of himself. Yet still he managed to have kindness in him.

She crossed the road and stepped into the shade of the magnolia grove. The scent of the blossoms hit her in a sweet, potent wave. He'd asked her for so little. He'd given her so much.

And when he had asked for something, she'd refused. Refused him the courtesy of listening to him, of listening and really hearing what he was telling her. She'd been too wrapped up in feeling sorry for herself. Too busy being certain she was being rejected to have empathy for anyone outside herself.

Anna began to run. She understood why Rush hadn't told her the truth when he'd first come to Ashland. She understood why he'd gotten angry with her last night.

Rush couldn't lay his heart or his hope out; he'd had both crushed too many times as a child. He'd learned to guard them. To protect them.

And he hadn't *planned* to get involved with her—just as she hadn't planned to get involved with him.

It had just happened.

It had been wonderful.

She loved him—everything he was. How could she be angry with him? How could she refuse to help him?

She couldn't.

Anna ducked out of the grove and cut across the lawn, heading straight for the overseer's house. She ran by a small clump of magnolias, dodging some low-hanging branches, heavy with blossoms.

A few feet past them, she stopped and went back. Breathing hard, she plucked one of the huge, snowy flowers to take to Rush, careful not to touch its petals. She brought it to her nose, inhaling deeply. Maybe, she thought, he would learn to love her. Maybe he would begin to feel he belonged here. And then he would want to stay.

Turning, she started to run again, closing the distance between her and the overseer's cottage in moments. She raced up the porch steps and pounded on his door.

When he didn't answer, she opened the door and looked inside. "Rush? It's Anna." Her voice echoed back to her.

Gone. He was gone. Panic rocketed through her, and she dragged in a ragged breath. Had he left for good? Without saying goodbye? Without giving her a chance to...

He hadn't. His duffel bag, obviously empty, lay across the old armchair. She brought a hand to her chest, making a sound of relief. Thank God.

Closing the door, she turned and went back to the porch, the blossom cradled in her trembling hands. As she sank onto a step to wait, she heard a pounding, like a hammer striking a nail. Standing, she followed the sound.

It led her to the gazebo. And Rush.

He'd ripped away the rotted ceiling boards and had begun replacing them with new ones. She tipped her head back and stared at him in surprise. "What are you doing?"

He looked down at her, his expression anything but pleased. "What does it look like I'm doing?"

She held a hand to her eyes to shield them from the sun. "Today is Sunday. Your day off."

"I took yesterday off." He slammed the hammer onto a nail.

"But only because I insisted."

He grunted in reply and reached for another nail.

She frowned as it finally registered what he was doing. "Rush . . . the gazebo wasn't on the repair list."

"I do know how to read."

"But—"

He looked at her. "You have a point here, Anna? I'm trying to work."

Realization dawned and her heart turned over. She lowered her eyes to the blossom, then lifted them back up at Rush. *For her. He was repairing the gazebo because she loved it.*

Warmth rushed over her. As did love. "I'll help you, Rush."

"Forget it. This is my project." He popped a couple of nails into his mouth and reached for another board.

"I'm not talking about helping with the gazebo. I want to help . . . you. I want to help with your search."

He stopped hammering and looked down at her, his eyes narrowed, his expression wary.

"Last night I was so wrapped up in my own feelings that I wasn't . . . sensitive to yours. Or to what you were telling me. I'm sorry. Of course, I'll help you. I'll do whatever I can."

For a full ten seconds, he stared at her. Then he set aside the hammer, climbed down the ladder and crossed over to her. Stopping in front of her, he searched her expression. A smile pulled at his mouth, and he motioned to the flower. "Is that for me?"

"Yes." Blushing, she held it out.

He took it and brought it to his nose, drawing in its fragrance as she had only minutes ago. He met her eyes over the flower. "It smells like you."

Her pulse stirred, and she looked away, uncomfortable and uncertain.

He touched her cheek, turning her face back to his. "I missed you, Anna."

"Did you?"

"God, yes."

He drew her against his chest, wet and musky-smelling with sweat. Her body responded to the scent, to his touch, with an almost frightening force.

She fought the urge to melt against him, and flattened her hands against his chest. "Look, Rush...you don't have to...thank me like this. I'm not a charity case."

He laughed and pressed his mouth to her throat. "Are you kidding?"

She wedged her arms between them. "No. I'm serious. I don't want us to be lovers...if you're... Not unless you really want..."

He cupped her face in his palms, searching her gaze. "How could you think I wouldn't want us to be lovers?"

"How could I not?" She pulled away from him, moving to stand several feet from him. She lifted her chin and met his gaze defiantly. "Look at me, Rush."

"I am. I have been." He closed the distance between them, and drew her back into his arms. "And what I see is unbelievably exciting. Feel how exciting I think you are.''

He took her hand and placed it against him. Even through his denims she could feel the strength of his desire. She made an involuntary sound of pleasure and curled her fingers around him.

"See, Anna," he whispered hoarsely. "I want you so much I'm crazy with it. All I have to do is look at you . . . think of you."

She whimpered and pressed closer to him. "Make love to me, Rush. Now. Here."

He kissed her—one long, drugging exchange after another. "Can't," he managed, his breathing ragged. "Sawdust. Splinters."

"I don't care."

She fumbled with his zipper, and Rush tugged her hand away. "Yeah, but you'd probably demand to be on top."

"You'll give me ideas," she whispered, looking up at him through partially lowered lashes.

At her provocative glance, he caught his breath and swept her into his arms.

"Where are you taking me?" she asking kissing his neck, nipping.

"I don't know. Any place that looks soft enough." He groaned as she stuck her tongue in his ear. "I swear, Annabelle Ames, if you don't stop that, I'm going to take you right now."

She lowered her gaze to the ruddy path, then laughed softly. "You wouldn't."

"Don't do it," he playfully growled. "I'm warning you, I mean it."

She ignored him, and tasted his ear again. Before she could even finish, he had her on the ground, lying on her back on the soft, petal-strewn path. He straddled her hips, and she looked up at him in surprise.

He laughed. "I told you before, I don't say what I don't mean."

"I'm sorry, Rush." She batted her eyelashes in exaggerated innocence. "I won't do it again."

"Too late, lady." He unfastened the first button of her shirt, then the next. And the next. He dipped his fingers under the gaping fabric and trailed it over the tops of her breasts.

Heat washed over her, and she curled her fingers into his damp T-shirt. "Your advances are most unseemly, sir."

He laughed and lowered his mouth until it hovered a fraction from hers. "Pay the price, babe."

"I demand to be on top," she whispered against his mouth. "I have sensitive skin."

"Do you?" His roving fingers brushed across a nipple. Anna caught her breath and arched. He laughed softly. "I guess you do. I'll take your request under advisement."

He finished unbuttoning her cotton shirt and parted the fabric. The warm breeze whispered across her flesh, cool compared to the fevered temperature of her skin. He unclipped her bra and cupped her breasts, moving his thumbs across the erect peaks.

Again she arched and moaned. "More?" he whispered, leaning down to taste her mouth again.

"Yes." She caught his mouth with her own. "More."

He did as she asked and when the time came, she returned the favor. Rush peeled away her shorts and shirt; she tugged at his jeans, pushing the damp denim over his hips. He rolled onto his back, taking her with him, so she straddled his hips.

His hands on her waist, he lifted her onto him. She arched her back as he guided her, the sensation incredible. Their skin grew slick with sweat; their breath came in short, ragged gasps. With a cry, Anna collapsed against him.

After a moment, he sat up and cradled her in his arms. ''I think there's a rock permanently embedded in my back.''

She reached around and stroked. ''My hero.''

''Stallion, you mean.''

He grinned wickedly, and she blushed, thinking of how she had just ridden him. ''That, too.''

His expression softened, his eyes filled with concern. ''I didn't scare you, did I? I worried, after I started this, that—''

She laid a finger against his lips. ''I never forgot, even for a moment, that it was you, Rush. And how could you frighten me?''

For long moments he gazed silently at her, then he smiled sadly. ''My sweet, sweet Annabelle.''

His gaze told her things she didn't want to acknowledge—not this moment—not ever. She curved her arms around his back, holding him tightly.

Her eyes lighted on the magnolia she'd brought him. It lay crushed on the path beside them. Tears stung her eyes, and she squeezed them shut. She had today. She had the summer. As foolish as it was, she would not give up the hope that he would fall in love with her and decide to stay.

Chapter Eleven

The days that followed were brilliant and hot; the nights, star-strewn and full of magic. She and Rush continued to make repairs to Ashland during the day. At night they searched for Rush's connection to the music box.

And they made love. All it would take was for one to look at the other and they would be in each other's arms, clinging, out of control. As they had that day on the path, they sometimes made love outdoors, underneath Sweethearts' Magnolia, or standing up, pressed against one of Ashland's side walls, or in the gazebo.

The days and nights had taken on the quality of an erotic dream, steamy and potent with the scent of flowers. A dream full of laughter as well as lovemaking, one full of sharing and tenderness.

Anna had never been so happy. In truth, she'd been happier than she'd ever thought she would be.

She stopped in the foyer just outside the parlor, a photo album held to her chest, and listened to the sound of Rush's voice as he talked on the phone. She smiled. His deep voice resonated through the house, filling the empty spaces, warming it—as he'd filled the empty spaces of her heart; as he'd warmed her.

Anna's smile faltered. Even though the time they'd spent together had been wonderful, she couldn't stop herself from worrying about where their relationship was going. Worrying about how long he would stay.

She stepped into the parlor. His eyes met hers, dark with awareness, and her pulse fluttered. Blowing him a kiss as she walked past, she settled herself on the settee. In the past week, he'd been in constant contact with Boston, with his business manager and several of his contractors. She'd been forced to face the fact that he had a life somewhere else. That he had friends and former lovers; that he had obligations, ties to a business and a community.

A life that didn't include her.

Anna clutched the photo album more tightly to her chest. In their time together, he hadn't spoken one word of love, hadn't made even a vague reference to a future together. He hadn't made her one promise.

And it hurt.

Why should she have expected otherwise? He'd told her not to get attached. He'd told her he left everyone behind.

But she'd hoped for a miracle. In her secret heart of hearts, she'd hoped he would find his connection to Ashland and feel compelled to stay.

She looked down at the photo album, one she'd found by accident, stored at the bottom of a box of her mother's old clothes. It represented the last of the photos. They'd gone through boxes of others, through drawers of old paperwork. They'd unearthed and read her grandmother's diaries and years of plantation ledgers. She'd begun making a list of the old-timers— people who had lived in Ames all their lives or had been friends of her family and might have some pertinent information for Rush.

Nothing had seemed to have a thing to do with Rush. It hurt to see his disappointment each time another avenue of their search didn't pan out.

She drew in a deep, painful breath. If he didn't find something, she knew, he would leave at summer's end as originally planned.

He didn't love her. There was no reason for him to stay.

Tears choked her, and she swallowed against them, scolding herself for her ridiculous hopes. She'd understood going in what a relationship with Rush would be. Whatever happened, it would be worth the pain.

She looked at him again, skimming her eyes over him. Arousal curled through her, a quickening of her pulse, a warmth that bloomed at the apex of her thighs and spread until she was aglow with it.

She flushed and jerked her gaze away from him. What was happening to her? They'd made love not two hours ago, and already she longed for him. She'd become like a junkie, craving his touch; she thought about making love all the time.

This power he had over her, frightened her. How would she go back to her old life? How would she go back to being Annabelle Ames, aging spinster?

How would she go on without Rush?

He hung up the phone and started toward her. Before he'd taken two steps, it rang again. He made an apologetic face, turned and picked it up.

Anna held her breath, wondering, as she did every time the phone rang, if it would be Lowell. She had expected him to call. She had waited, a knot of worry in the pit of her stomach. But she hadn't heard a word from her brother since the night he had come to see her. Neither had Macy or Travis.

Anna let out her pent-up breath as Rush began a conversation with the person on the other end of the line. It clearly wasn't her brother calling.

She shifted her gaze to one of the dark windows. What was her brother doing? Was he all right? She'd considered calling the police; had considered it many times over the past days. And more often than that, she'd wondered if she'd done the right thing when she'd turned him away. She didn't know.

"Dammit." Rush dropped the phone into its cradle.

She looked at him. "What's wrong?"

"That was Pete Garner. His father had a stroke."

"Hayward? Oh, no." Anna sat up straighter. "How is he?"

"Critical. But his doctor thinks his chances of pulling through are good."

"Thank God."

Rush rubbed a hand wearily across his forehead. "But he's not coming to Ames. Obviously. I won't even be able to talk to him, probably for months. If then."

Anna stood and went to him. Wrapping her arms around his waist, she pressed her face into the crook of his neck. She ached for him; ached seeing his hopes dashed yet again.

She tipped her face up to his. "I'm sorry, Rush."

For long moments he gazed at her, then he bent his head and kissed her. Slowly, deeply. And with a wealth of emotion that left her breathless.

He lifted his head; tears choked her. His kiss, the emotion behind it, had touched the core of her. She felt as if he'd shared the most special and private part of himself with her. Something he would never consciously do.

"Thanks for understanding."

She smiled. "My pleasure."

He motioned to the settee. "Found another album?"

"Mmm." She dropped her arms and took a step away from him. "With some of Mama's things."

"No diary, though?"

Anna shook her head. "She must not have kept one."

Rush made a sound of frustration and dragged his hands through his hair. "Another brick wall. Maybe I'm not supposed to know. Or maybe this whole thing has been a ridiculous figment of my imagination."

"I don't believe that. Neither do you."

"No?" He met her eyes. "How can you be so sure?"

"Because you were so sure, Rush. Because you not only recognized the music box, you knew the tune before it played." She grinned. "You're not a man given to flights of fancy or wild imaginings."

A smile pulled at his mouth. "You know that about me, do you?"

She laughed. "Yeah, I do."

She went to the settee and sank onto it. She patted the place next to her. "Let's take a look. You never know, this may be the one."

He crossed the room, bent down and kissed her, then took a seat beside her. Anna snuggled closer against his side, and laid the album across their laps. She opened it and they began leafing through. Anna recognized pictures of her father as a young man. She recognized her grandparents, some friends of the family. She pointed out who was who as they turned the pages.

"Who's this?" Rush asked, stopping at a photo of two young men. They were mugging for the camera, each with an arm thrown around the other's shoulders.

Anna squinted at the grainy photo. "That's Daddy, on the right." She tilted her head, considering the other young man. He was considerably bigger than her father, very good-looking. "I don't know who the other guy is. There's something familiar about him, but I'm not sure."

"Maybe it's labeled." Carefully they loosened the photo from its paper mount, then turned it over.

Joshua and Robert. July, 1939.

"Robert who?" Rush muttered, frustrated.

Anna frowned. "I don't know. Let's look some more. Maybe there are some other pictures of the same guy."

They continued to thumb through the half-full album, finding a handful more photos of people Anna didn't recognize. She carefully extracted those, as well. The last photos in the album depicted her father and mother after they were first married.

They found no more photos of the unidentified Robert.

Rush picked up the bunch of photographs they'd taken out of the album, and studied them. He narrowed his eyes, looking at the blurry images in the photos. Could one of these unidentified men be his father? One of the women his mother?

He tossed the photos down, stood and strode to one of the windows. He'd never encountered anything so frustrating in his entire life. He felt like he was looking for the needle in the proverbial haystack. He was surrounded by bits and pieces of things that could be clues, but how the hell was he supposed to recognize them?

"Funny," Anna murmured suddenly.

Rush turned from the window and looked at her. Head bent, she stared down at the open album.

"What's funny?"

She looked up. "These are pictures of Mama and Daddy when they were first married."

"So?"

"So, there are no pictures of her."

"Who?"

"Daddy's first wife."

He couldn't have heard right. Rush took a step toward Anna. "Your father was married before?"

"I wouldn't even know about her except I overheard Macy and Mama talking about her once. I don't even know what her name was. They weren't married very long. A couple of years."

Rush's heart began to pound. And he was a couple of years older than Anna. "What happened to her?"

Anna lifted her shoulders. "She died. I don't know how. Daddy remarried soon after."

"Why didn't you tell me this before?"

She stiffened, and he could see by her expression that he'd offended her. "I wasn't trying to keep anything from you. It never crossed my mind." She glanced down at the album once more. "Until I saw these early pictures of Mama and Daddy."

Joshua Ames had been married once before. Good God, this could mean...

His palms began to sweat, the blood to thrum in his head. Rush crossed to the settee. "Anna?"

Something in his voice must have alarmed her, because her head snapped up, her eyes on his wide with concern. "What?"

"Could your father's first wife have died in childbirth? Could she have borne him a child?"

Anna caught her breath. "A son?"

"Could she have?"

"No." She shook her head, eyes widening in shock. "No, she couldn't have."

"How can you be sure? Isn't it feasible?"

"I would have heard about it. I would know...that."

"Would you? Don't you think it's a little strange that you had to *overhear* your mother and Macy talking about your father's first wife? Why would it be such a big secret? And don't you think it's strange that there are no pictures of her?"

"No." Anna cocked her chin. "I don't think it's strange at all. Daddy was probably brokenhearted when she died. Mama probably didn't like being reminded of Daddy's first love. It makes perfect sense."

"Very romantic interpretation, Annabelle. Especially considering what you've told me about your parents."

She balled her hands into fists. "I don't know how you can even consider this a possibility! That would make me...it would make us—"

She bit the words back and lifted her chin. "Why would Daddy discard his own son, Rush? Why?"

Rush swore. "You're right. I'm sorry. This whole thing is making me crazy."

"I know." She reached up and caught his fingers. He squeezed them, then swung away from her, going back to the window and the night beyond.

He stared out at the dark. Something was nagging him, something just beyond his reach. Turning, he crossed to the drawing of Lowell and Anna picnicking under the magnolia. He gazed at it, frowning. They were missing something, something right under their noses. Something obvious.

He blinked, his vision clearing. He saw his own face reflected back at him in the drawing's protective glass.

The drawings! Of course!

He swung to face Anna once more, his heart thundering. "Didn't you say your mother recorded your lives in her sketches?"

"Yes. For as long as I can remember, she..."

Rush saw the realization dawn in Anna's eyes. "Of course your mother didn't keep a written diary, Anna. She kept a visual one instead."

Anna pressed a hand to her chest, to her runaway heart. "My God. How could we have missed that?"

"Are these framed pieces the only drawings there are?"

Anna shook her head and jumped up. "No. There are at least a dozen sketch pads in storage up on the third floor."

Their eyes met. Without speaking, they raced up the two and a half flights of stairs to the third-floor storage area.

Anna had been wrong. There weren't a dozen tablets, there were nearly fifty of one kind or another. They were dusty, some of them mildewing.

"Let's take them downstairs," Rush said, gathering up an armload. "It's too hot to breathe up here."

It took three trips for them to transport all the pads to the parlor. After they had, they sat on the floor, with the tablets scattered out around them.

Anna glanced at Rush. He looked nervous, his features drawn, his jaw tight. He met her eyes, then reached for one of the tablets. He opened it. The pages were fragile with age. Carefully, he flipped them.

As he did, Anna narrated. She recognized her father. Brady and Macy. The plantation as it had been in the old days. The images brought tears to her eyes.

"Who's this?" Rush asked, stopping on a lovingly rendered drawing of a little boy with huge eyes and a solemn expression. The boy looked to be about two.

"I don't know."

She saw Rush's excitement. She felt it. Her own adrenaline began to pump through her, leaving her light-headed and shaking.

He flipped quickly through the sketch pad until he came to another of the same boy, this time holding an infant on his lap. In this one the boy was smiling.

Rush looked at Anna. She narrowed her eyes and shook her head. "I'm not sure. About either of them."

He muttered an oath and started flipping through the tablet again, in his haste ripping several of the delicate pages. He stopped as the little boy's face stared back at them once more. Again, the child held an infant, only this time Anna recognized herself as the baby.

"That's me!" she said excitedly. "I'm sure of it. Remember, there was a photo of me in the same bonnet."

"What about the boy?"

"I don't know. I don't... Wait a minute."

"What is it?"

She looked at Rush, stunned as a memory from her childhood sprang full-blown in her head. "I just remembered . . . I was maybe seven or eight, I'd been going through Mama's vanity. I remember finding a photograph of me and a little boy. When I showed Mama the photograph and asked who he was, she became very upset. Near tears, if I remember right. I guess I recall that now, because Mama didn't scold much. She almost never spanked."

"But she did this day."

Anna nodded. "She took the photo away and sent me to my room. I never saw it again."

"Did she say who the boy was?"

"No." Anna shook her head. "But it might not even have been the same boy."

"But it could have been?"

"Sure."

They dug into the sketch pads, searching through each one, not taking the time to study or admire. The boy was never depicted again.

Frustrated, Anna tossed the last pad down. "Why didn't she label any of these? People label photographs, why not drawings?"

Rush gazed at that first drawing, the one of the boy alone. "Who do you think he was?"

Anna shifted her gaze to the drawing. "The child of a family friend. Maybe even one of the plantation workers. We can start checking my list of names and make some calls. Macy and Brady are due back from Memphis. She might know."

"You really think this boy was a friend of the family?"

"Sure." Anna looked at her hands. They were filthy, dusty, her fingers smeared with charcoal and pastel. She stood to go wash them. "Who else could it have been?"

He lifted his gaze to hers. She saw what he was thinking and shook her head. "No way."

"How do you know, Anna?"

"Because I do." She took a step backward. "Daddy didn't have any other children."

Rush stood and faced her. "But what if, Anna? That would mean you and I—"

"No!" She started for the kitchen, the adrenaline of panic pumping through her. When she reached it, she crossed to the sink and flipped the water on. Rush had followed her, and she looked over her shoulder at him. "Why would he send his own son away?"

"True." Rush let out a long, frustrated breath. "Why would he? That would make him some sort of monster."

Anna caught her breath. That was Lowell's description of their father. It always had been.

Stunned, she met Rush's gaze. In his she saw a similar thought. A similar fear. Her stomach turned. It couldn't be. It was too farfetched to be true.

But if it was true...

Rush would be her half brother.

Anna grabbed the bar of soap. She lathered her hands, furiously scrubbing at them, tears welling in her eyes. But it wasn't true. It wasn't.

"We have to find out, Anna." Rush came up behind her. She felt his breath on the back of her neck, felt the heat of his body. She longed to lean against him. Longed to find comfort in his arms, his mouth.

Hysteria bubbled up inside her. But she couldn't—maybe never again.

He placed his hands on her shoulders, massaging the tight muscles. "We have to be sure, Anna. You see that, don't you?"

She whirled on him, shaking with anger. With helpless fury. "I see, all right. I see that you hope it's true. You hope Daddy is your father."

Rush took a step back from her, his expression stunned. "What?"

"Finding out who you are means more to you than I do. It always has. Even if it means finding out I'm your...that we're...brother and..." Her voice broke, and she turned back to the sink, to scrubbing her hands.

It was too awful. Too terrible. But she had a sick feeling in the pit of her stomach that it was true.

Good God, what would she do? That would mean she was in love with her brother. That she'd...made love with..."

"This is crazy, Anna." Cupping her elbow, Rush turned her to face him. "You're talking crazy—"

"Am I?" She lifted her chin, tears sliding down her cheeks. "You were always more interested in Ashland than in me. More interested in your connection to this place than in me."

He shook her. "Anna, stop it! This is a shock for both of us, but we don't know anything for sure yet. The child might be what you thought—a friend of the family. A distant relative. There might not even be a connection between me and Ashland."

She pulled away from his grasp. "You don't believe that. I know you don't. Besides, that's not what this is about. I'm talking about us. I'm talking about your feelings for me."

"Where is this coming from?" He closed the distance she'd put between them, and cupped her face in his palms. "Anna, the last thing I want to discover is that we're so closely related. My God, I don't know how I would live with that."

She made a sound of pain and curled her wet soapy hands into his pullover. She pressed her face to his chest. She wanted to kiss him so badly the want clawed at her. She wanted to make love with him. But she couldn't. And she was afraid.

He pressed his lips to the top of her head. "We'll get through this, Annabelle. I swear we will."

She lifted her gaze to his, tears slipping down her cheeks. "But what will be waiting for us on the other side?"

"I don't follow."

She drew in a deep breath, her lips trembling so badly she could hardly form the words. "Do you love me?"

"Annabelle—"

"Do you?" He tried to move away from her; she tightened her fingers. "I love you. I've fallen in love with you."

He shook his head. The panic in his eyes would have been laughable had it not cut her so deeply. "You don't love me," he said. "You love what we do together. You love that you can finally be with a man and respond." He touched her cheek, stroking gently. "You don't love me. I promise you don't."

Anna fisted her hands against his chest. He didn't want her to love him, she saw that now. He didn't want the complication. The strings. "Like a patient who falls in love with her shrink? You think what I feel for you is some sort of transference? Bastard!''

She lifted a hand to slap him; he caught it. A muscle jumped in his jaw but his eyes were dark with regret. With pain. "I didn't want to hurt you. I didn't mean to."

Fresh tears rolled down her cheeks. "What are your feelings for me, Rush? Besides the obvious physical ones?''

He released her and crossed to stand by the window. For long moments he stared out at the black, then he turned back to her. "Wasn't I honest about my feelings, Annabelle? Did I once say something that led you to believe this was forever? I don't operate that way. Forever's not even in my vocabulary.''

"And that doesn't answer my question."

"It's the best I can do."

Anna drew in a shocked breath, seeing the truth in his eyes, but not wanting to believe it. She shook her head. "You don't even know, do you? You're so scared of feeling anything, you wouldn't know love if it smacked you in the face."

He reached a hand out to her. "I like you, I enjoy being with you. Lord knows, I love making love with you. But I don't know where my feelings for you end and for Ashland begin. I don't know how to separate what we have between us from what I feel about being here. Maybe they can't be separated."

Her breath caught in a sob, and she covered her face with her hands. Once again her relationship with a man had been tainted by Ashland. Once again, she hadn't been wanted for herself alone.

He took a step toward her. "I'm sorry, Anna. I didn't mean to hurt you."

Angry, she backed away. "You said that before."

"I don't know what else to say."

Standing ramrod straight, she lifted her gaze to his. "If you can't say you love me, just say goodbye."

For one impossibly long moment he hesitated, his gaze on hers torn. Then, without saying anything, he turned and walked away.

When she heard the front door snap shut, Anna curled her arms around herself and cried.

Chapter Twelve

In her dream the phone was ringing. Anna opened her eyes, realizing that the ringing wasn't part of her dream. Disoriented, she uncurled herself from her position on the settee, moaning as her muscles and spine screamed their displeasure.

Her foot was asleep, and she limped across the room to the phone. "Hello," she managed, her voice sounding like sandpaper.

"Anna? Is that you?"

"Yes." She cleared her throat. Her head pounded from crying and she didn't have to look into a mirror to know her eyes were swollen and red. "Who is this?"

"Pete Garner."

"Pete?" She pushed the hair away from her face, her head beginning to clear, the memory of her last meeting with Rush filling it. Pain took her breath.

"Anna, listen." For the first time, she heard the worry in the doctor's voice. "Riverview Memorial just called. Your brother's been brought into the E.R."

"Lowell?" She shook her head. "At Riverview?"

"He's in bad shape. Apparently, somebody worked him over pretty good."

They're going to break my legs, Anna. You've got to help me.

Her brother's words resounded in her head and she gripped the sideboard to steady herself. He hadn't been lying, Anna realized. He hadn't fabricated the story to try to manipulate her into selling Ashland. And she'd turned him away. She'd turned her brother away.

"Anna, are you still there?"

"Yes," she managed. "What did they... How bad—"

He cut her off. "I don't know the specifics. I suggest you get there as soon as you can. I'll meet you."

"No, Pete, wait! You have to tell me.... How bad is..."

The doctor had already hung up. Anna stared at the buzzing receiver, tears blinding her. She brought a hand to her mouth. Lowell had begged for her help. She'd turned him away.

Now, he was in the hospital.

A sob caught in her throat, and she dropped the receiver into its cradle. She needed her keys, she thought, looking frantically around her, hysteria clawing at her. She needed her purse. Where had she left them?

She raced to the kitchen, flipping on the overhead light, squinting and making a sound of pain as she did. She found her purse and rifled through it for her keys, swearing when they weren't there. She dumped the purse's contents on the kitchen table to be sure, then swore again.

Where were they? Where—

Rush, she remembered. Rush had used the truck that afternoon.

Throwing her purse back together, she ran out the back door and across the dark yard. She reached the overseer's house in moments and pounded on the door. "Rush! It's me, open up!" She pounded again. "Please... open up!"

"Anna! My God, what's wrong?"

She swung around. Rush stepped out of the shadows and started up the porch steps. She looked at him through a veil of tears, wishing she could throw herself in his arms, wishing he could comfort her. "The keys," she managed. "Do you have the truck keys?"

"Yeah." He fished in his pocket and pulled them out. "But what's—"

Anna snatched them from his hand. "I've got to go."

"Go? Anna..." As she rushed by him, he caught her elbow. "It's the middle of the night."

She jerked against his grasp. "It's Lowell. I've got to go."

She freed herself and ran to the truck. She yanked the driver's side door open and climbed inside.

"Wait!" Rush caught up with her. He grabbed the door, preventing her from shutting it. "What do you mean, it's Lowell? What's going on?"

She gasped for breath as she struggled to fit the key into the lock. "He's at Riverview Memorial's emergency room. He's hurt.... I've got to go to him."

"I'll drive you."

"No." She shook her head. "I don't need your help."

"You're hysterical, Anna. Slide over." When she resisted, he added, "How much good are you going to be to your brother if you end up in a ditch?"

She swore and acquiesced. He climbed behind the wheel and started the old vehicle up. "You'll have to give me directions."

She did and within moments they were whizzing down the highway that connected the community of Ames to that of Riverview.

Anna stared out the window, unable to see for her tears.

"You want to talk about it?" Rush asked.

"It's my fault," she whispered, not looking at him. "He told me this was going to happen. I didn't believe him."

Rush glanced at her from the corner of his eye. "Told you what was going to happen?"

She filled him in, covering her face with her hands when she'd finished. "What am I going to do if he...? I'll never forgive myself if..."

"It's not your fault." Rush reached across and squeezed her hand. "You didn't get him into trouble. You can't blame yourself."

"You don't understand," she said, slipping her hand away from his. "You just don't understand."

Rush's jaw tightened into a hard line. "No, I guess I don't."

They didn't speak again and by the time they reached the emergency room, Pete Garner was already there. He nodded at Rush and hugged her.

"Are you okay?" he asked.

"I'm fine." She drew in a shaking breath. "What about Lowell?"

The doctor guided her over to a deserted grouping of chairs. He sat across from her, while Rush positioned himself behind her chair. "He's in surgery, Anna. He's bleeding internally. They have to find the source and stop it."

"Oh, my God..." Anna brought a hand to her mouth.

"Luckily, a couple out necking found him in a ditch on Lovers' Lane. He was unconscious when they brought him in, and he hasn't regained consciousness yet."

Anna curved her arms around herself. This couldn't be happening, she thought. Not to Lowell. Not to her baby brother.

"I'm not going to lie to you, Anna. I'm not going to sugarcoat it. Both his legs are broken, one of his arms. All his ribs are either broken or fractured. His skull looks okay, thank God."

Pete Garner leaned toward her. "He's alive, Anna. He was found in time. You've got to focus on that."

She nodded dumbly, struggling to get a grip on herself, her emotions. She felt Rush's steady presence behind her, felt his quiet strength. He dropped a hand onto her shoulder, reassuring, and she reached up and covered it with her own.

She drew in a deep breath. "How long was he...out there?"

"About twelve hours. It could have been a lot worse. Whoever did this, knew exactly what they were doing. They knew just where to hit him, just where to hurt him. They didn't want to kill him. Not immediately, anyway."

I made enemies of the wrong guys, sis.

You've got to help me. I've got nowhere else to turn.

Her breath caught in a sob. She'd turned him away. Guilt and grief wound through her until she didn't know where one began and the other left off. If it even mattered.

The hours passed with excruciating slowness. Lowell made it through surgery, although he didn't regain consciousness. Night gave way to day, and finally they let Anna in to see him, but only for a moment. At the sight of his battered face and body, at the myriad of tubes and machines, she'd had to fight not to fall completely apart.

Rush stayed with her, although Anna found it a mixed blessing. He brought her coffee, forced her to eat a bite or two of a doughnut. His presence was comforting, but the distance between them was an agony. She wanted him to hold her; she wanted to lean on him, wanted to know he loved and supported her.

She wanted the impossible. And it hurt like hell.

Midmorning, Travis rushed into the waiting room. "Anna! I just heard."

Anna ran to him, flinging herself into his arms. He hugged her tightly, and she pressed her face to his chest. "It's so awful, Trav. His face . . . He's so broken. . . ."

"Is he conscious?"

Anna shook her head. "No, not yet. They've patched him up, found the bleeding and stopped it. He should have come around, but he . . . hasn't."

Travis stroked her hair. "Have you called Macy?"

Again, Anna shook her head. "She's at her sister's. She'll be back in a couple of days. I thought that would be soon enough to tell her. We'll know more then."

Travis muttered an oath. "Who did this to him, Anna? Who would want to hurt him?"

Anna started to cry—great racking sobs that she couldn't control. Travis stroked her hair, murmuring sounds of comfort.

Rush watched them, jealousy twisting in his gut, a biting sense of alienation with it. He flexed his fingers and dragged his gaze away. He wanted to be the one to hold and comfort her. He wanted to be the one she turned to.

He had no right. She wanted more from him than he could give.

"Miss Ames." The nurse came into the waiting room, all smiles. "Your brother's awake."

"Awake." Anna squeezed her eyes shut and drew in a shuddering breath. "Thank God."

"How is he?" Travis asked. "Is he . . . all right?"

"He's foggy yet," the nurse replied, "but he appears to be lucid. Give us a few minutes and you can see him."

Rush watched as Anna threw her arms around Travis once more, the jealousy and alienation growing and swelling until he had to fight for an even breath.

On the outside again. Always on the outside.

He turned away from the pair and crossed to the waiting room's picture window. After their argument, should he expect anything else? He'd been unable to give her what she wanted—what she'd needed. He'd been unable to love her.

He'd hurt her.

Love. He pressed the heels of his hands to his eyes. In the twelve hours they'd been at the hospital, he'd seen a myriad of emotions play across Anna's face: joy and grief, fear and hope. Anger.

The fact that she loved her brother was unquestionable.

Unquestionable, too, was the fact that she would do anything she could to help him.

Even after the way he'd hurt her, again and again.

Was that what love was?

Brother and sister. He looked at Anna, this time at her reflection in the glass. His chest tightened. Could they share the same blood? Could they unwittingly have committed such a grievous sin against nature?

Rush curled his fingers into fists, despair rising like bile inside him. He'd told himself no. He'd told himself he couldn't have responded so sexually to his sister. It should be a genetic impossibility.

He knew it wasn't.

The picture window faced the parking lot, and Rush gazed at the activity below, at people rushing in for care or to see loved ones, at the hospital staff coming and going.

After he'd left Anna the night before, he'd been unable to sleep. He'd been disturbed by their argument, haunted by the image of the young boy in the drawing. So he'd walked the plantation grounds, looking within himself for answers.

The boy from the drawings was him. He knew it in his gut, in his heart. When he had looked into that child's eyes, he'd seen himself, the man he would become. The one he had become.

And the boy hadn't been the child of family friends. Or even a distant relative. Rush had read that fact in the drawing, in the loving way the child had been rendered, in emotional sensitivity the artist had seemed to have to the subject.

Rush frowned, his gut tightening. Anna's mother hadn't drawn outsiders. In all the other sketch pads, the only people depicted were those living on the plantation.

The answer seemed devastatingly obvious.

He hadn't pointed that out to Anna. He hadn't wanted to upset her anymore and besides, they would have proof soon enough.

But why, if he was Joshua Ames's son, had he been sent away? It had crossed his mind that Anna's mother might have been jealous; he'd discarded that notion the moment he'd really looked at the drawing. Whoever the boy had been, Constance Ames had loved him very much.

Rush drew his eyebrows together. It was ironic. He'd waited so long to discover who he was, and now was so close to realizing the truth, yet he found no joy in it.

He wished he'd never started searching.

The nurse poked her head into the waiting room and called Anna. Rush looked over his shoulder, and Anna's gaze found his. She smiled brilliantly, and his heart turned over.

Had he ever loved? he wondered, turning back to the window. The way Anna loved Lowell? The way she professed to love him?

He tightened his fingers. He had. A long time ago.

Emotion choked him; he battled it. If this ache of helplessness and alienation was love, who needed it? If loving hurt so much, what was the point?

Rush stiffened. He should have left the past alone. He shouldn't have come here. Why had he cared about finding his past? It didn't matter—not really. It wouldn't change him, wouldn't change his life.

He would leave Ames, go back to Boston. As soon as Anna was on her emotional feet.

A woman came into the waiting room directly behind him. She was petite, with a cap of flame-red curls. Rush squinted at her reflection in the window. He would recognize her anywhere.

It was Marla from Small Miracles.

Rush caught his breath. What was she doing here?

He swung around, her name on his lips. The waiting room was empty except for Travis. The other man arched his eyebrows coolly.

"Where did she go?" Rush asked.

"In to see Lowell. He woke up."

Rush shook his head, impatient. "Not Anna. The other woman. With the red hair. She was just here."

"I didn't see anybody."

"But I...saw her...in the...glass." Rush frowned and shook his head. "Never mind."

"I don't think so."

Rush narrowed his eyes as Travis crossed the waiting room. "Excuse me?"

The other man stopped before him. "Hurt Anna and I'll kill you."

Travis uttered the threat quietly, but with a wealth of meaning. Rush hadn't a doubt the man meant what he said. Rush met his eyes, unperturbed. "That's a pretty bold statement for a guy in a thousand-dollar suit."

"I don't give a damn about the suit. It's Anna I care about." He took a step closer to Rush. "Hurt her, and I'll kill you."

Rush swept his gaze over Travis Gentry. He had six inches and fifty pounds on the other man. Yet Travis was threatening him.

The truth hit him like a blow. Anna needed a man like Travis Gentry. Solid and dependable. A man who could love her. A man able to make a commitment.

At the thought of Anna with this man, or any other, fury rushed over him. Jealousy with it. Rush flexed his fingers, battling the emotion. "She must mean a great deal to you."

"More than a man like you could understand."

Rush narrowed his eyes. He wanted to flatten the guy. He wanted to tell him that Anna's welfare was none of his concern, that he had it well in hand.

He couldn't do that. He'd hurt her already. His relationship to her might make that kind of possessiveness unthinkable.

And when he left, she would be better off with Travis.

The thought took his breath. "I'll consider myself warned, Gentry. Excuse me."

Anna sat beside Lowell's bed, battling tears. By the time she'd made it to his side, he'd fallen asleep. So she'd sat quietly beside him, holding his hand and praying.

It hurt to see him this way. It hurt to know she could have prevented this.

He meant more to her than anything. Certainly more than Ashland. He was her brother. She curved her hand around his, laying so still and white against the hospital sheet. He'd been right about her, she realized. She'd used Ashland to hide from life for too long. She'd let Ashland substitute for love. She'd used it to hide her, protect her, comfort her.

No more.

She loved her brother so much. To help him, she would sell Ashland—without a moment's regret. It was, after all, only mortar and brick.

She bent and pressed her cheek to their joined hands. What would he say when he saw her? Would he remind her that she'd turned him away? Would she see blame in his eyes when he looked at her? She didn't know if she could live with it if he did.

"Hey, sis."

Anna lifted her head. Lowell had awakened and looked at her, his swollen eyes barely slits. Her own eyes filled with tears. She fought back a sob. "Hey, baby brother."

Lowell smiled weakly, the curving of his mouth almost a grimace. "What's with the tears?"

They welled and slipped down her cheeks. She brushed at them, feeling completely helpless. "What do you think?"

"You don't like my new look?" He coughed, the sound weak and ragged. "It's the latest from Bad Guys 'R' Us."

This time she couldn't catch the sob, and she buried her face in her hands. "I'm so sorry. So sorry, Lowell. Please forgive me." She met his eyes, brushing at her tears. "You mean a million times more to me than Ashland. I'll sell, Lowell. I don't want it if it means you're going to be hurt again."

"Anna...you didn't...do this."

She curved her fingers around his, clinging. "But if I hadn't refused to help you...if I hadn't—"

"You'd have sold Ashland and I'd still be a weak, worthless piece of trash."

She looked up. His voice had been so faint, she wasn't certain she'd heard correctly. "What...did you say?"

"That you were...right." He coughed again. "You can't sell our heritage. You can't sell what you...love so much."

"But, it's only a thing, Lowell. It's only—"

"I've messed up my life. Done my best to mess up yours. I've treated you so badly, you probably don't even know...how much I...love you."

"Oh, Lowell. I love you, too."

He grasped her fingers, squeezing weakly. "I'm not...like...Daddy. I'm going...to prove..."

His eyes fluttered shut and his grip on her fingers eased. He'd fallen asleep again. Anna leaned over to kiss his cheek, and found that it was wet.

Her heart turned over; her own eyes filled. She hadn't seen him cry since he'd been a boy.

She brought his hand to her mouth and kissed it. "I love you," she whispered. "You're going to be okay. Finally, you're going to be okay."

After several minutes, she carefully slipped her hand from his and stood. Her first thought was of Rush. She wanted to tell him what had happened, wanted to share the good news with him.

But he was gone.

Anna moved her gaze over the nearly empty waiting room, the taste of disappointment bitter in her mouth. She looked at Travis. "Where's Rush?"

"He left."

"Oh." Tears stung her eyes, and she looked away. "I see."

"How's Lowell?"

"Sleeping now. But..." A tremulous smile pulled at the corners of her mouth, and she looked back at her old friend. "But he's okay, Trav. In a way he hasn't been in a long time." She clasped her hands together. "He's going to try to get his act together."

Travis dragged a hand through his hair. "Thank God."

Exhausted, Anna sank into a chair and leaned her head against its back. She closed her eyes.

"Anna?"

She didn't look at him. "Hmm?"

"We need to talk."

She opened her eyes and met his gaze. She saw what was coming in his expression. She didn't want to face it, not now when she was so emotionally and physically drained. But it wasn't fair to keep Travis hoping.

She straightened. "Yes, Trav?"

"Have you thought anymore about my offer?"

She hesitated at his word choice. *Offer.* As if he'd made her a business proposition. He wasn't in love with her, Anna realized. Not even a smidgen. Knowing that made what she had to do easier. "You mean your marriage proposal?"

"Yes."

"I have," she said softly, carefully. "But my answer hasn't changed. I can't marry you, Travis."

He let out a pent-up breath, disappointment marring his handsome features. "I'm sorry to hear that."

She stood and crossed to him. She gathered his hands in hers. "I'm in love with Rush."

"And does he love you?"

The question hurt. Because Rush didn't, and because she suspected Travis knew that. But he had asked anyway.

Anna inched her chin up. "Do *you* love me?" she countered.

"You know I do."

"I know you love me as a sister. As a friend. But that's not the same thing. And you know it."

He shook his head. "We could have a good marriage, Anna. We have so much in common. We're so much alike."

She looked him in the eye. "Truthfully, Trav, which do you want more? Me or Ashland?"

"That's not fair."

"It's very fair." She reached up and stroked Travis's cheek. "I don't want to be a part of a package deal. I want somebody to love and want me for *me*. And only me. I want romantic love. I want passion."

"And you have this with Cousins?"

"Yes."

Travis started to turn away from her. She caught his hand again, lacing their fingers. "Someday you're going to meet a woman who absolutely sets your pants on fire. You won't want to be married to your comfortable old friend, then. If I told you yes, we would both end up hurt. I don't want to lose you, Trav. You're too important to me."

He smiled and brought her hand to his mouth. "I don't want to lose you, either."

"Can we still be friends?"

"You haven't given me any other choice." He squeezed her fingers to take the sting out of the words, then released them. "I hope this guy makes you happy. You deserve it."

Tears filled her eyes. "He won't. He doesn't love me back."

"I'm sorry, Anna."

She smiled sadly. "Me, too, Travis."

Chapter Thirteen

Anna spent the next several days at the hospital, only returning to Ashland to shower and sleep. Lowell continued to improve, and as he did his resolve to change didn't waver. He'd even talked to Travis about a job. Anna had never seen him so determined before. She believed that finally he would turn his life around.

But what of her own life? she wondered, gazing out her bedroom window at the brilliant new morning, finding no joy in it. She hadn't seen Rush since that first day at the hospital, although she'd seen lights on at his house and evidence that he'd been working on Ashland during the day.

She'd missed him. She'd ached for him. That wasn't going to change.

Anna turned away from the window. Over the past days, whenever she'd begun to despair over her relationship with Rush, she'd thought of something else, anything else. She'd immersed herself in Lowell's needs, spending long hours at the hospital, pushing herself until she was exhausted. And it had worked.

But she couldn't go on this way. She couldn't ignore or deny her feelings any longer. Anna headed out to the hall and down the stairs. She had to know if Rush was her brother or not. And once she did, she would know the right way to say goodbye.

Tears choked her, and she fought them back. Now wasn't the time to fall apart. She would have plenty of time for that in the days and weeks ahead.

Anna crossed the foyer, stopping at the parlor doorway. Her mother's sketch pads were still spread out over the floor. Taunting her.

Who was that little boy? she wondered, gazing at the tablets. Was he Rush? Her stomach tightened into a knot of denial. She didn't want it to be true, but wishing it wasn't so wouldn't change the truth. And it wouldn't make the problem go away.

Anna walked into the parlor and sat on the floor. She picked up the sketch pad that contained the drawing of the boy and opened it. For long moments she gazed at the drawing, studying the boy's face.

Who was he?

Macy would have the answers they sought. She'd returned from her sister's the day before and had visited Lowell at the hospital. Anna hadn't mentioned anything about Rush or the drawings; then hadn't been the time or place.

Now was.

After calling Macy to arrange a time to stop by, Anna gathered up the drawing tablet and went in search of Rush.

She found him at the toolshed, getting out the equipment needed for the day's repairs.

He stopped what he was doing and watched her approach. He looked tired and tense. And unbearably sexy in his white T-shirt and blue jeans.

"Hi," she said softly, wanting to touch him but clasping her hands tighter around the tablet instead.

He looked down at the ground, then back up at her. "How's Lowell?"

"Doing well. He's...doing very well. Thank you."

Rush smiled. The curving of his lips looked stiff, uncomfortable. "I'm glad for you, Anna."

Silence stretched between them. Terrible and leaden. Would it always be this way between them? she wondered. No matter the outcome of their meeting with Macy, would it always be so awkward?

She took a deep breath. "I called Macy this morning. She said we could come by."

She heard his quick intake of breath, and she knew she'd surprised him. "Are you sure you want to do this?"

"Yes." She looked away, her throat closing over the words. "We have to know, Rush. I realize that now. A part of me, a big part, wants to stick my head in the sand and hide from the truth."

She shook her head. "But I can't do that. I've done it for too long. I've used Ashland to hide from life, to hide from the real world. Lowell was right about that."

She drew in a deep breath. "It's scary, though. I'm not going to lie about that. The emotional ramifications of this are so...far-reaching. My feelings for you are involved, what we've been to each other. My feelings for my father...maybe even my mother. Who knows?"

"I'm sorry I came here, Anna. I'm sorry I hurt you."

The pain in his eyes tore at her. She took a step toward him, her own eyes swimming. "You changed my life. You've given me so much." She shook her head. "Please ... don't regret having come here. Don't regret our having become lovers. Before you, I was lonely. And afraid. Of being touched. Of being hurt."

She stroked his cheek with her fingertip, then dropped her hand. "Before you, I thought I'd never be able to love a man."

"Anna—"

She stopped him. "I *do* love you. The way I feel isn't about sex." She brushed at a tear that slipped from the corner of her eye. "Considering what we suspect may be possible about our relationship to each other, it sounds almost obscene to tell you how I feel. But I wanted to tell you now, before we meet with Macy, because after...I might not be able to. I love you, Rush."

He folded her into his arms and held her. Quietly. Without touching her in any other way. And she clung to him, knowing that this could be the last time she held him as her lover.

Squeezing her eyes tightly shut, she tried to memorize this moment, its sensations. His rich, male scent, the thrum of his heart against hers, the whisper of his breath against her hair. Soon, memories would be all she had.

She drew away from him, searching his features. "Ready?"

He smiled and nodded. There was a youthful eagerness in his expression that tore at her heartstrings. He'd waited a long time for this. She prayed he found his answers today.

They walked to the truck in silence, and save for Anna giving Rush directions, they didn't speak again until they'd reached Macy's house.

Macy opened the door, her big face wreathed in smiles. When she saw Rush, she didn't try to hide her surprise. "Why, Annabelle, I didn't know you were bringin' a friend."

Anna smiled. "You remember Rush?"

"'Course I do." Macy beamed at him. "The Yankee. Come on in."

She led them to the parlor, then went in search of another teacup and cookie plate, despite Rush's assurance that he didn't care for anything.

It seemed an eternity, but finally they were all seated, facing one another. Beside her, Anna heard Rush suck in a deep breath. She glanced at him and saw the impatience that pushed at him. Felt his excitement. She could understand. This could be the day he finally caught up with his past.

Or it could be nothing.

Her stomach twisted into a dozen different knots. As if sensing her unease the way she'd sensed his, he reached across and squeezed her cold hand.

Macy watched them, a perplexed expression on her face. She shifted her gaze to the sketch pad in Anna's hands. "Why, Annabelle, that looks like one of Miz Constance's sketch pads."

"It is," Anna said breathlessly. "It's why we've come today."

Macy nodded. "I knew somethin' was up. Tell old Macy what it is."

Anna opened the tablet to the drawing of the boy and handed it to Macy. "Rush and I found this and we were wondering . . . hoping, you would know who this boy is.''

The older woman gazed at the drawing, tears filling her eyes. She lifted them to Anna. ''Where did you find this?''

''On the third floor with the rest of Mama's tablets.''

Macy shook her head. ''I don't believe it. I thought Mr. Joshua had done away with all of these.''

Rush reached for her hand again, this time clinging to it. Anna choked back a sound of despair. ''Why would Daddy do that? Who was this child?''

''This was my boy,'' Macy said softly, her dark eyes filling with tears. ''And your mama's.'' The tears slipped down her cheeks and she brushed at them. ''Lord knows, I haven't been able to gaze at this sweet face in so long.'' She stroked the edges of the paper lovingly. ''My little Robby.''

''Robby who?'' Anna pressed. ''Why don't I know him?''

For several moments, Macy remained silent, studying the image before her. Then, as if preparing herself for an ordeal, she drew herself up and looked straight at Anna. ''You know your daddy was married before?''

Anna nodded.

''Miz Cecelia was one pretty woman. Dainty as a flower, an' sweet as one, too. Full of life. But she wasn't strong like your mama. No, sir, she wasn't strong at all.''

Macy sighed and looked at the drawing once more. ''As you know, Mr. Joshua wasn't the easiest man to live with. He was terrible moody an' given to wild, reckless behavior. He was downright mean many a time. Those two should never have married. I knew it all along but no one bothered to ask Macy.''

The old housekeeper's eyes glazed over as she remembered. ''They weren't married but a couple of months before Miz Cecelia knew she'd made a terrible mistake. She was cryin' all the time. Sick from bein' so sad. Mr. Joshua started takin' off for long stretches, months at a time. It was during one of those stretches that Cecelia turned to his best friend, Robby, for comfort.''

''Robby?'' Rush asked, leaning forward.

''Robert Lee Truesdale. He was Joshua's first cousin by marriage. Sweet boy. Gentle. Big and good-lookin', too. Like you are.''

The photo. Anna looked at Rush; she saw by his expression that he remembered, too. That's why the man in it had seemed familiar, she realized, her heart pounding. He'd reminded her of Rush.

''One thing led to another,'' Macy continued. ''Your daddy found out about the affair when Cecelia was almost at term with Robby's baby. We all known it wasn't Mr. Joshua's child, that it couldn't be. He would have too, if he'd counted back.''

The old woman folded her big hands tightly in her lap. Anna knew how difficult this must be for her; she could see the pain in her eyes. ''Even with all his moods, I'd never seen Mr. Joshua like that before. He went crazy. Insane with jealousy and rage. Couldn't blame him his feelings none. He'd been betrayed by both his wife and best friend. And all along preparin' for the baby, and thinkin' it was his. But still, the good Lord didn't create us in His likeness to act that way. No, sir.

"He and Miz Cecelia fought. In all my days I'd never heard such a terrible row. Nor have I since." Macy shuddered. "Me an' the other house girl, there wasn't nothin' we could do 'cept listen in horror. After all, we were servants. An' black ones at that. He hit her at least once. I know, 'cause I heard her hit the wall."

Macy shook her head sadly. "An' her with child, too. I knew it would cost me my job, but I couldn't stand it no more and was runnin' to call the sheriff, when Mr. Joshua, he yelled for me.

"Miz Cecelia had gone into labor. Your daddy, he stormed off, leavin' me and the other girl to tend her. In those days the closest hospital was Greenville, and I knew she didn't have time to make it there. Doc Garner took care of us all, but he was over in Riverview seein' to another woman. So I sent Brady to fetch him an' called the midwife. Many a baby had been born by midwife, and I thought..."

Macy lowered her eyes to her hands, folded as if in prayer. After several moments of silence, she began again. "I believe Miz Cecelia would have made it had Doc Garner been there. But the midwife, she couldn't stop the bleedin'. An' by the time the doc did get there, she was too far gone. Like I said, Miz Cecelia wasn't a strong woman."

"Oh, Macy..." Anna reached across and covered her old friend's hand. "How horrible for you."

"I wished I could've done more..."

"What about the baby?" Rush asked quietly.

"A fine, healthy boy," Macy murmured, lowering her eyes to the tablet. "This boy."

"But, Macy," Anna said, drawing her eyebrows together in confusion, "what happened to him? He didn't grow up at Ashland, yet in these drawings he's at least two.''

"I'd just lost my own little baby, and I still had milk. It was decided that the baby would live with me and Brady until he was weaned. Then he would be given up for adoption.''

Her voice thickened with tears. "Then along came Miz Constance. She fell in love with that little boy. We all did. 'Cept Mr. Joshua. He hated him.''

Macy met Anna's eyes. "After the thing with Miz Cecelia, your daddy was never the same again. His moods became blacker, he drank and gambled all the time. He insisted the child be named after his real daddy, although I never knew why. It was almost as if he wanted to be reminded of... what had happened.

"Your mama, she didn't want to let her little Robby go. But she came to realize she had to. She had another baby to consider—you, Annabelle—and she knew Robby wouldn't grow up right at Ashland. Because of Joshua's hate. And she hoped that Mr. Joshua would begin to forget.'' She shook her head sadly. "Me and Brady wanted to keep him. But it wouldn't have been proper, us being black.''

Tears stung Anna's eyes. Macy had always wanted to be a mother. But because of the color of her skin, she hadn't been able to keep a child who had loved and needed her. Senseless and sad.

"Mr. Joshua had assured your mama that he'd found a good family up north for Robby, and he took him away. For a while he was better. Then along came Lowell and it started all over again. His black, bitter moods. His binges.'' She lifted her shoulders. "It was as if his own son reminded him of the one that hadn't been his.

"Miz Constance mourned her little Robby for the rest of her days, finding comfort only in the fact that he was in a good home with parents who loved him.

"I mourned him, too," Macy said, turning her gaze to Rush, tears slipping down her cheeks. "You that little boy?" she asked. "You my little Robby?"

Rush gazed at her, his eyes bright. Anna saw his fight for control. "Yes," he said, his voice rough with emotion. "I believe I am."

She held out her arms. "Then come here, child. I been waitin' a long time to hold you in my arms again."

Rush hesitated a moment, then stood and went to her. The big woman folded her arms around him, and after a moment, Rush wrapped his around her, too. Anna watched, choked with emotion, tears running down her face.

Macy opened her eyes and held out her other arm. "You, too, sugar sweet. Come to your old Macy."

Anna did, and for a long time they just held each other. Finally Macy eased her hold on them, and sat back against the couch. But she held on to Rush's hand. "The Lord answered my prayers," she murmured. "I prayed I would see my little boy one time before I died."

She shut her eyes for a moment, and Anna could see how their visit had fatigued her. Rush must have too, because he said gently, "We should leave you to rest, Macy."

She opened her eyes and held on to his hand. "I have to know," she said softly, her eyes full of hope. "Did your parents treat you right? Were they good people?"

Rush squeezed her fingers and smiled gently. "They were wonderful people. They loved me more than anything."

The old woman smiled and leaned her head against the couch once more. She released Rush's fingers and sighed. "My little Robby. Who would have thought he'd come back to me?"

He stood and gazed down at her, his expression softer than Anna had ever seen it.

Anna bent and kissed Macy's damp cheek, and she and Rush crossed to the door. There, she turned back to her old friend. There was a question she had to ask, one that wouldn't wait until Macy had more energy.

Macy must have seen it in her expression because she motioned at her with her right hand. "Ask me, sugar sweet. I'll answer if I'm able."

"Is there any chance that...Daddy really was Robby's father? Any chance at all?"

Macy shook her head. "Your daddy took off for weeks and months at a time. One time he didn't come home for nearly four months. That was when our little Robby was conceived. Considerin' the baby's birthday there was no question."

Anna drew her eyebrows together. "But how had she planned to...explain that to Daddy?"

"Don't think she did, sugar sweet. I think she and Robby planned to run away together." Macy shook her head. "Soon after, Robert disappeared. Heard tell he joined the army and got killed in Korea. His folks didn't have much, and they moved away not long after."

So sad, Anna thought, softly closing the door behind them. Tragic. Those three adults had messed up their lives royally, but the one who had paid for it was Rush.

Anna bit her bottom lip. And what of her father? How could the man who had told her stories of Southern gentlemen and codes of honor have behaved in such a reprehensible manner? He'd lied to his wife, to Macy. He taken out an act of vengeance on an innocent child. And how would she ever be able to think of him again and not shudder?

Anna glanced at Rush from the corner of her eye as they walked to the truck. "Thank you," she said softly. "For not telling Macy the truth about your life. It would have broken her heart."

"I never want her to know the truth," he said grimly. "Never."

They didn't speak again, and as the truck ate up the miles between Macy's and Ashland, the silence became more and more deafening.

What was he thinking? Anna wondered. What was he feeling? She tried to put herself in his position, but found she couldn't.

She hugged herself. She ached. For people and events of the past that she couldn't change; for a future she feared she couldn't shape; and for the man she loved, whom she didn't know how to comfort.

She reached across the seat and touched his arm. "How do you feel?"

He glanced at her, then looked back at the road. A muscle worked in his tight jaw. "I don't want to talk, Annabelle. I need a little time to . . . sort it all out."

Hurt speared through her, and she drew her hand away. He was shutting her out. His next move would be packing his bag for Boston.

Minutes later they pulled into Ashland's long, winding drive. Rush parked the truck, but neither of them made a move to get out. Anna stared at her hands, clasped in her lap. "When you do know how you feel, look me up. I think the least I deserve is a goodbye."

Not trusting herself to look at him without bursting into tears, she opened the door, slipped out and walked away.

The new day had dawned clear and bright. Rush stood at the edge of his front porch and gazed at Ashland. Over the past few days he'd done his best to sort through what he'd learned about his past. He'd gone back to the Ames *Gazette,* to the microfilms. There, on the society pages, he'd found pictures of his mother. And of his father.

He saw no physical resemblance between himself and Cecelia Ames, but in some of the photos his resemblance to Robert Truesdale, his father, was striking. Disconcerting, even, because looking at the photos he knew beyond a shadow of a doubt, that this man, this stranger, was his father.

But still, he'd studied them with a certain detachment. These people had given him life but had never been a part of his life. What was he supposed to feel for them?

Rush curved his fingers around the porch railing. And he thought about Joshua Ames and his hatred. And he'd wondered about that trip he'd taken up to Boston with him, wondered if he would ever remember. Or if he even wanted to.

He'd talked to Macy every day, learning more with each conversation about the boy he had been, about what his life had been like at Ashland.

And during it all, Anna's question had played over in his head—*How do you feel?*

How did he feel? As if a great weight had been lifted from him. He felt a tremendous sense of relief to finally know; a terrible sadness for the two people who had given him life.

And he felt an incredible sense of joy to know that he had been loved.

That meant more to him than anything else. It filled him with light and warmth. It made him feel, at last, free of the past. At last whole.

Rush smiled and drew in a deep, sweet breath. He had no desire, no need, to probe any deeper into his past. He had no want to find his biological family.

He'd done what he'd come to do. There was no reason for him to stay.

Except Anna.

His heart swelled. Anna had worked magic on him. He'd never known a woman like her before. It had taken her, and this place, to show him how rootless he was. And how much he longed for those roots. How much he missed them.

He loved her. With everything he was and would be. He loved her more than he'd ever thought himself capable of loving.

It felt wondrous. Miraculous and new.

Rush looked toward Ashland again. He missed her. He ached to hold her, to talk to her. How had he been so blind? How had he not seen what she meant to him?

Because he'd allowed the past to hold him back. Because he'd allowed fear of being hurt to control him. Because he hadn't been whole.

He was now. Now, he understood love. Now he was able to love.

If only it wasn't too late.

Heart pounding, he started for the house. And Anna.

Anna stepped out onto the gallery, Blue at her side. She walked to its edge and gazed out at the grove of magnolias. It had been three days since she and Rush had gone to Macy with her mother's sketch pads. Three days since she'd talked to Rush. Three days of emotional agony.

She'd left the ball in his court, although she didn't believe his next move would be much of a surprise. He didn't love her. He would leave, go back to Boston and the life he had known there.

And her life would never be the same.

Blue barked and bounded down the stairs. Anna turned in the direction he'd gone, her heart pounding, her mouth dry.

Rush rounded the house. She watched him as he stopped to scratch Blue's ears, then start toward her once more. She feasted her eyes on him, knowing it was probably one of the last times she would be able to do so.

He climbed the steps, crossing to where she stood. He didn't speak, didn't smile, and she clasped her hands in front of her. Her chest tightened and she fought for an even breath. This was it, she thought. This was goodbye.

He spoke first. "The other day you asked me how I felt. I didn't know then. I was still in a sort of shock. I know now."

"Oh?" She swallowed. Hard.

"I love you, Anna."

She took a surprised breath. "What?"

"I love you. I want to stay with you."

Tears stung her eyes, and she shook her head. "You don't love me. You love Ashland."

"No." He caught her hands. "It's not Ashland. It's you. For the first time in my life, I feel like I belong. I—"

The tears spilled over, and she tugged against his grasp. "For a long time I prayed you would find your connection to Ashland and want to stay. I thought that would be enough for me. But it's not enough."

"Anna—"

"No, let me finish. I want to be loved for me, Rush. Not for this place. I deserve to be loved wholly and without strings."

He pulled her back to him. "It's not some *place* I belong, Annabelle. It's with some*one*. It's with you." He cupped her face in his palms. "With you and by your side is where I'll always belong. No matter where we are. Belonging isn't about a place. It's about love."

She searched his expression, her heart thundering in her chest, a cautious hope blooming inside her. She slipped out of his grasp and went to the edge of the gallery. For long moments she stared out at the grounds. Then she turned back to him. "How do I know that's the way you feel, Rush? How can I be sure it's me and not Ashland?"

"You have to trust me, Annabelle." He held out his hand. "Trust me."

She gazed at his outstretched hand, her heart thundering in her chest. All she had to do was grasp it. So simple. So natural.

"Trust me," he murmured again. "Trust me."

The breath shuddered past her lips. The joy burst into full bloom inside her.

He loved her! Wholly and without strings. He loved her as she'd always dreamed of being loved; as she deserved to be loved.

With a cry of happiness, she flew across the gallery and caught his hand. His fingers closed over hers—strong, dependable. Loving.

She tipped her face to his, meeting his steady gaze with her own. She would never look back. Never wonder.

"I love you, Rush."

He smiled. "I love you, Annabelle."

Turning, they went together into Ashland.

Epilogue

Boston's Boylston Street bustled with activity. Rush looped an arm around Annabelle's shoulders, chuckling at her wide-eyed enthusiasm. "So, do you like it?"

She laughed. "Isn't it obvious? I love it!" She shook her head, then tipped her face up to his. "It's so different from the South. Everything about it—the buildings, the people, the air, even."

"There's Small Miracles." Rush pointed to a brownstone across from them. "Come on."

They ducked across the street, earning the blare of a horn from a disgruntled taxi driver. "Do you think she'll be here?" Anna asked. "I can't wait to meet her."

"I'm certain she will. I don't know why, but I am."

They climbed the steps to the shop, opened the door and stepped inside. There they stopped, startled. Marla sat on the dainty settee Rush remembered from his last visit, the silver tea service on the table in front of her, a cup in her hand. Otherwise, the shop was empty.

She looked up when they entered, smiling brilliantly. "Welcome! Come in, come in. I've been waiting."

She waved them inside and after exchanging an amused glance with Anna, Rush led her across the room. He smiled. "I don't know if you remember me—"

"Of course I do. Rush Cousins. I never forget a client." She smiled again and turned her amazingly blue eyes to Anna.

Rush began the introductions. "Marla, this is Annabelle Ame—"

"From Ashland Plantation," the pixieish woman finished for him. "And aren't you lovely, too? Happiness is so good for the complexion."

Anna smiled. "Thank you. It's a pleasure to meet you."

"We've come to thank you," Rush said, curving an arm around Anna and drawing her closer to his side.

"Thank me?" the tiny woman repeated. "Whatever for?"

"For bringing us together." Anna caught Rush's hand. "If he hadn't found you and the music box, we wouldn't have found each other."

Marla clapped her hands together. "But how wonderful." She stood and came around to them. Standing on tiptoe, she kissed their cheeks. "I wish you all the happiness and love in the world."

She stepped back from them, a hand over her heart. "Love is so... inspiring. To see such nice young people come together, well . . ." She shook her head. "It almost makes me regret that I'm getting out of the miracle business. But, I've earned my wings. So to speak." She laughed. "And it's time for a vacation. Someplace warm, I think."

"You're closing your shop," Rush murmured, feeling a pang of regret. "You had some beautiful things."

"I did, at that. Although I believe the music box was my most...exquisite of all." She led them to the door. "I'll miss my Small Miracles but I'm looking forward to my vacation. I do so love to fly."

After thanking Marla again, Rush and Anna stepped out into the bright and busy day. Rush caught her hand. "So, what did you think of my leprechaun?"

"Good fairy," Anna corrected. "And you were right, she is strange. But in such a...warm way. She left me almost breathless."

Rush laughed as they descended the stairs. "She does have a way with that." He checked his watch. "Do you think Sandy, Joey and Shaun are okay? Maybe I should call. They haven't been with us that long, and I don't want them to—"

"They're fine." She squeezed his hand. "Travis seemed pretty excited at the prospect of being foster daddy for a weekend."

"Maybe I should call anyway."

She laughed and shook her head. "We called before we left the hotel. They were doing great."

"You're right. It's just that I want them to be . . . happy with us. Do you think they are?"

Anna stopped and lifted her face to his. "I think they're very happy. And I think you're the best foster daddy in the whole world."

Emotion choked him, and Rush leaned down and kissed her. "I love you, Annabelle Ames."

"Cousins," she whispered against his lips. "Annabelle Cousins."

* * * * *

HARDHEARTED
Bay Matthews

Chantal Robichaux would rather die than call on Dylan Garvey again, but now she desperately needed his help. Chantal's newborn baby—a baby Dylan didn't know was his—had been kidnapped. If anyone could find their son, it was tough cop Dylan. Dylan's heart, on the other hand, would be hard to reach...and only Chantal's love could soften his defenses.

Share Chantal's loving reunion in Bay Matthews's HARDHEARTED, available in January.

THAT SPECIAL WOMAN! She's friend, wife, mother—she's you! And beside each Special Woman stands a wonderfully *special* man. It's a celebration of our heroines—and the men who become part of their lives.

TSW194